THROWING GAUNTLETS

Fargo snapped. In the blink of an eye he had the Colt out and up and slammed the barrel against Landreth's head.

"Lord Almighty!" the hardcase called Tucker bleated. "Did you see that? I hardly saw his hand move."

"I'm serving notice," Fargo said to all of them. "The next son of a bitch who gets in my way better have a hankering for the hereafter." He twirled the Colt into his holster and looked at Moon. "How about you?"

"If I decide to, I'll pick the time and the place. This ain't it."

Fargo took a stride but Moon wasn't done.

"One more thing. If and when I do decide, it won't be in the back. I am a lot of things but not a back-shooter."

Fargo remembered him shooting the unarmed driver, and wasn't impressed.

"Anytime you want."

THE
TRAILSMAN

#341

SIERRA
SIX-GUNS

by

Jon Sharpe

A SIGNET BOOK

SIGNET
Published by New American Library, a division of
Penguin Group (USA) Inc., 375 Hudson Street,
New York, New York 10014, USA
Penguin Group (Canada), 90 Eglinton Avenue East, Suite 700, Toronto,
Ontario M4P 2Y3, Canada (a division of Pearson Penguin Canada Inc.)
Penguin Books Ltd., 80 Strand, London WC2R 0RL, England
Penguin Ireland, 25 St. Stephen's Green, Dublin 2,
Ireland (a division of Penguin Books Ltd.)
Penguin Group (Australia), 250 Camberwell Road, Camberwell, Victoria 3124,
Australia (a division of Pearson Australia Group Pty. Ltd.)
Penguin Books India Pvt. Ltd., 11 Community Centre, Panchsheel Park,
New Delhi - 110 017, India
Penguin Group (NZ), 67 Apollo Drive, Rosedale, North Shore 0632,
New Zealand (a division of Pearson New Zealand Ltd.)
Penguin Books (South Africa) (Pty.) Ltd., 24 Sturdee Avenue,
Rosebank, Johannesburg 2196, South Africa

Penguin Books Ltd., Registered Offices:
80 Strand, London WC2R 0RL, England

First published by Signet, an imprint of New American Library,
a division of Penguin Group (USA) Inc.

First Printing, March 2010
10 9 8 7 6 5 4 3 2 1

The first chapter of this book previously appeared in *Hannibal Rising*, the three hundred
fortieth volume in this series.

Copyright © Penguin Group (USA) Inc., 2010
All rights reserved

The Trailsman

Beginnings . . . they bend the tree and they mark the man. Skye Fargo was born when he was eighteen. Terror was his midwife, vengeance his first cry. Killing spawned Skye Fargo, ruthless, cold-blooded murder. Out of the acrid smoke of gunpowder still hanging in the air, he rose, cried out a promise never forgotten.

The Trailsman they began to call him all across the West: searcher, scout, hunter, the man who could see where others only looked, his skills for hire but not his soul, the man who lived each day to the fullest, yet trailed each tomorrow. Skye Fargo, the Trailsman, the seeker who could take the wildness of a land and the wanting of a woman and make them his own.

California, 1859—A storm is coming to Hell Creek. . . .

1

Skye Fargo liked the Sierra Nevada Mountains. They were miles high. They were remote. Lush forest covered the lower slopes, snow capped the high peaks.

Unlike back East, where much of the wildlife had been killed off to fill supper pots, animal life was everywhere. Ponderous grizzlies were on perpetual prowl, tawny mountain lions glided through shadowed woodlands, hungry wolves roved in packs. Elk, deer, mountain sheep and a host of smaller creatures were the prey the predators fed on.

On a sunny autumn morning, Fargo drew rein on a switchback on a mountain no white man had ever set foot on and breathed deep of the crisp air.

A big man, he wore buckskins and a white hat brown with dust. A red bandanna around his neck had seen a lot of use. So had the Colt on his hip and the Arkansas toothpick snug in an ankle sheath. His eyes were as blue as a small lake below. His beard was neatly trimmed.

Fargo gigged the Ovaro. He was on his way to San Francisco and had decided to spend a week or so alone in the high country. He liked to do that every now and then. It reminded him of why he enjoyed the wild places so much.

Fargo loved to roam where no one had gone before. Where most men kept their gaze on the ground and the next step they were about to take, his gaze was always on the far horizon. He had to see what lay over it.

A game trail made the descent easy. A lot of creatures came to the lake daily to slake their thirst.

Fargo was almost to the bottom when he spied two does. They jerked their heads up but they weren't looking at him. They stared intently at a thicket that bordered the shore. Suddenly wheeling, they bounded off, their tails erect.

Fargo wondered what had spooked them. It could be just about anything. Deer were easily frightened. Still, to be safe, he reined up and watched the thicket. A minute went by and nothing appeared so he clucked to the Ovaro and rode to the water's edge. Dismounting, he let the reins dangle, and stretched. He had been in the saddle since sunup.

Sinking to one knee, Fargo dipped a hand in the lake. The water was cold and clear. He sipped and smacked his lips. "How about you, big fella?"

As if the stallion understood, it lowered its muzzle.

"Not too much now." Fargo had a habit of talking to the stallion as if it were a person. Often, it was his only companion for days at a time.

The stallion went on drinking.

High in the sky a bald eagle soared. In the forest a squirrel scampered from limb to limb. Out on the lake a fish broke the surface. The day was peaceful and perfect, exactly as Fargo liked them.

Then the Ovaro raised its head and pricked its ears and nickered.

Fargo looked and froze.

A dog had come out of the thicket. A huge dog, almost four feet high at the front shoulders and bulky enough to weigh upwards of two hundred pounds. It had a blunt face with a broad jaw and a thick barrel of a body. Its color was somewhere between brown and gray. At the moment it was standing still, its dark eyes fixed intently on him.

"Hell," Fargo said. Where there was a dog there were bound to be people and he had hoped to fight shy of them for a spell.

The dog took a step and growled.

Fargo smiled and gestured. "I'm friendly, boy. You'd be wise to be the same." Out of habit he placed his hand on his Colt. He wasn't worried. If the dog came at him he could drop it before it covered half the distance.

From behind him came the crack of a twig.

Fargo glanced over his shoulder.

Another dog, the same breed and about the same size, had emerged from the woods. Its hackles were raised and its lips were drawn back. Its teeth looked to be wickedly sharp.

"Damn." Fargo didn't like this. He stepped to the Ovaro and snagged the reins and was about to slip his boot into the stirrups when a sound caused him to whirl.

A third dog wasn't more than ten feet away. Its huge head held low, it crouched.

"Down boy." Fargo scanned the shore for sign of the owner but saw no one.

He quickly mounted. He figured to get out of there before the dogs decided to attack.

The nearest dog moved to a point between the stallion and the woods, blocking his way.

"Son of a bitch." Fargo was trying to recollect where he had seen dogs like these before. Then it came to him: Saint Louis, some time back. Mastiffs, they were called. He seemed to recall they were bred in England or some such place but he could be mistaken.

The dog to the right and the dog to the left moved slowly toward him.

"Go away, damn you." It occurred to Fargo that if they rushed him he might drop one or two but not all three, and all it would take was one to bring the Ovaro down. He didn't dare risk that. Suddenly reining toward the lake, he used his spurs.

The stallion reacted superbly, as it nearly always did. It took a long bound and plunged into the water.

Fargo bent forward and hiked his boots out of the stirrups.

The Ovaro would swim to the other side and he would be on his way, no worse for the bother. He chuckled, pleased at how he had outwitted the dogs, confident they wouldn't come after him. He shifted in the saddle to be sure.

All three mastiffs jumped in. The nearest surged swiftly after the Ovaro, swimming with powerful strokes, its head high, its teeth glistening in the sunlight.

"Damn dumb dogs." Fargo was growing mad. He'd tried to spare them, and now look. He drew his Colt and took aim but changed his mind and holstered it. So far, the Ovaro was holding its own. If he could stay ahead of them until he reached the other side, he could get away. The dogs might be fast but over a long distance the Ovaro's stamina would win out.

The bottom of Fargo's pants was soaked. He would have to dry them and his boots and socks later. But at least his saddlebags and bedroll were mostly dry. The Henry in the saddle scabbard was getting wet and he would have to dry and clean it later, a chore he could do without.

Fargo checked behind him. The nearest dog hadn't gained any and the others had no chance in hell of catching him before he struck solid ground.

Several ducks took noisy wing, frightened by the commotion.

The dogs didn't give up.

Fargo wished he knew who their owner was. He'd pistol-whip the bastard for letting them run free. It made him wonder what anyone was doing there, so far from anywhere.

The Ovaro swam smoothly, tirelessly.

Fargo's gaze drifted to the shore they were making for and a tingle of alarm rippled down his spine. "It can't be."

A fourth dog had emerged from the forest and was pacing back and forth, waiting for them.

"What is this, the whole litter?" Fargo grumbled. He reined the stallion to the right. The mastiff on the shore moved in the same direction. Fargo reined to the left. The dog moved to cut him off. Once again Fargo drew the Colt. He had nothing against dogs but he would be damned if he'd let them attack him. As soon as he was close enough, the beast on shore was dead.

They were awful well trained, Fargo reflected, and was struck by a hunch. He scoured the vegetation and was about convinced his hunch must be wrong when a shadow detached itself from a tree. He couldn't see clearly enough to tell if the figure was white or red but since Indians seldom had mastiffs he took it for granted it was a white man and hollered, "Call your damn dogs off!"

The shadow didn't respond.

"Did you hear me?" Fargo raised the Colt. "Call them off or you'll bury them."

The figure stepped into the open.

Fargo half wanted to pinch himself. "Lord Almighty," he blurted in amazement.

It was a woman. She couldn't be much over twenty. Luxurious red hair cascaded over her slender shoulders, framing an oval face as lovely as any female's ever born. Her clothes consisted of a homespun shirt and britches that might have been painted on. She had an hourglass shape and a full bosom, and was barefoot. One hand was on her shapely hip and in the other she held a six-gun that she now trained on Fargo. "You shoot any of my dogs, mister, and I'll sure as blazes shoot you."

Fargo's mouth moved of its own accord. "Then call them off, you idiot."

The girl's face became as red as her hair. "You best keep away, you hear? We don't cotton to strangers. It's ours and ours alone."

"What is?"

"I've said all I'm going to." The redhead put two fingers to her mouth and let out with a piercing whistle. Immediately, the dog on the shore turned and trotted toward her.

Fargo looked back. The dogs in the lake were veering toward her, as well.

5

He turned toward the forest again—and she was nowhere to be seen. "What the hell?"

Fargo was tempted to go after her himself but he had the Ovaro to think of. He continued on, and presently the stallion had solid ground under its hooves and was out of the lake and dripping wet.

The three dogs bolted into the woods as soon as they were out of the water.

"So much for them," Fargo said in mild disgust for the inconvenience they had caused. He resumed his interrupted journey. When he reached the far end of the lake, he stopped and glanced back, seeking some sign of the girl and her pack. He wondered who she was. A homesteader, he reckoned, which meant a cabin must be nearby. It bothered him. He never expected to find another living soul this deep in the mountains.

With a shrug, Fargo clucked to the stallion. He had never been in this particular part of the Sierra Nevadas before and he was eager to explore. A fir-covered slope brought him to a ridge. He stopped to look down at the lake and blinked in surprise.

The girl and her dogs were staring up at him.

Fargo smiled and waved. It might do to show her he could be as friendly as the next gent.

The girl pointed up at him and said something to the dogs and all four bounded up the slope.

Fargo couldn't believe this was happening. It looked as if she had sent her pets after him. Cupping a hand to his mouth, he shouted, "What the hell are you doing? Call them back! Now!"

The girl just stood and stared.

Swearing lustily, Fargo hauled on the reins and used his spurs. He went down the far side of the ridge and came to a narrow valley.

Bursting from the woods, he stuck to open ground and brought the stallion to a gallop. There was no way in hell the mastiffs could catch him now.

Half a mile of hard riding brought Fargo to a bend. He thundered around it and abruptly drew rein, dumfounded by the unexpected sight that unfolded before him.

To the north reared broken bluffs, a creek meandering along their base.

To the south along the flank of the valley were over a score of buildings, most made from planks and a few from logs and the rest slapped together using whatever was handy. A single street dotted by several hitch rails and a water trough ran the length of the town.

"I'll be damned." Fargo had no inkling he was anywhere near civilization. So far as he knew, there shouldn't be a town or settlement within a hundred miles.

Hell, make that two hundred. He tapped his spurs and rode closer and the truth dawned.

The street was thick with dust. One of the hitch rails was broken and the water trough was dry. The wear and tear of neglect showed on every building; roofs sagged, windows were broken, overhang posts had tilted or were cracked. Moved by the breeze, a single batwing on a saloon creaked noisily.

It was a *ghost* town.

Fargo rode to the near end of the street and drew rein. A small sign, faded but readable, told him the town's name. "Kill Creek," he said out loud. He rose in the stirrups and surveyed the creek and spotted a long-abandoned dredge. The dredge explained everything.

Back in 'forty-nine gold was at Sutter's Mill. A horde of people from all over the country and from all walks of life flocked to the California mountains hoping to strike it rich. That so few ever did didn't deter them. Each thought they would be the one. Thousands more came to provide food and lodging and whatever else the gold seekers needed.

Towns sprang up virtually overnight. All it took was for someone to find a nugget or two, or pan a poke's worth. Word would spread like a prairie fire.

Almost always, the new strikes were short-lived, and once

7

there was no more gold to be had, the horde moved on to the next strike. In their wake they left abandoned towns and deserted camps.

Kill Creek was one of those towns.

That Fargo never heard of it didn't surprise him. There were dozens just like it, forgotten and empty of everything save bugs and dust.

He rode down the street until he came to the creaking batwing. It wouldn't hurt to rest a spell. He was about to climb down when something squeaked and a rat came scuttling from between two of the buildings, ran out into the middle of the street, promptly wheeled, and ran back into the shadows again.

"It's my day for stupid animals," Fargo said, and chuckled. It died in his throat the very next moment.

Around the bent at the other end of town loped the four huge mastiffs.

Running shoulder to shoulder, their sleek muscles rippling under their hides, they made straight for Kill Creek.

And for him.

2

There was only so much Fargo would abide. It was bad enough the dogs had chased him into the lake and then had the gall to jump in after him. Now here they were again, evidently intent on taking up where they had left off.

"Not if I can help it," Fargo said, and shucked the Henry from its scabbard. He hadn't had time to clean it yet but it should work just fine. He levered a cartridge into the chamber and wedged the stock to his shoulder. Taking a deep breath to steady his aim, he went to aim.

The mastiffs were gone.

Fargo raised his head. They had been there not two seconds ago. He figured they would reappear and stayed ready to shoot but nothing happened. Tired of waiting, he slowly rode up the street. The dull thud of the Ovaro's hooves and the creak of his saddle were the only sounds. Otherwise the ghost town was eerily still.

Fargo went to the end of Kill Creek and didn't see the dogs.

Reining up, he debated what to do. Common sense said to light a shuck but his curiosity was percolating like hot coffee. He'd like to learn more about the redhead. Most of all, he would like to learn how she looked without her shirt and britches. Grinning, he returned to the hitch rail in front of the saloon, swung down and looped the reins.

The inside was no different from the outside. Dust was

everywhere. Some of the chairs were on their sides and the only table had been overturned. Floorboards were broken and split. The pine bar had been scratched and gouged and had bullet holes. He walked behind it. He didn't figure on finding anything to drink but he groped the shelves anyway and was unfurling when the gleam of glass from under the bar caught his eye. Squatting, he leaned the Henry against the wall and slid his hand underneath. He felt a strange tickle on his skin.

The tickle moved.

Fargo pulled his hand out, and froze. A black widow was crawling over his knuckles toward his sleeve, her black belly swollen and distended like the belly of a woman nine months along. Black widow bites didn't always kill but it would make him sick as could be. He stayed still until her legs were on his buckskins. Slowly turning, he smacked his sleeve against the wall, squishing the widow like an overripe grape.

Fargo flicked the gob off and reached under the bar. His fingers made contact with the neck of a bottle. Pulling it out, he held it up to a shaft of sunlight streaming in the broken window. "I'll be damned." It was half full. He opened it. The label had been peeled off but he knew what it was from the color and the smell and confirmed it with a quick swig: whiskey.

Fargo smiled. He took the bottle over near the window and righted the table and a chair. Plunking the Henry down, he sat where he could watch the Ovaro and see a good portion of the street, and propped his boots up. He treated himself to a full swallow, chuckled and let out a contented, "Ahhhhh."

Fargo warmed his gut with a few more chugs, then set the bottle on the table. He didn't want to drink it all at once. It would be days before he got to have more.

He thought about the mysterious redhead and her dogs. She must live in Kill Creek. What she was doing there was anyone's guess. He doubted she had stayed on after the town died. Not by her lonesome. A filly that pretty, he speculated that she must have a man or a family close by. Which brought him back to his original question: What in hell was she doing there?

Fargo sighed and sipped. He would stay a while and see if she turned up. Could be she was as curious about him as he was about her. By the sun it wasn't much past ten. He would wait until noon and if she didn't show he would continue on his way.

Half an hour went by. The quiet got to him. It was like sitting in a cemetery late at night with tombstones all around and that feeling that something might rise up out of a grave.

"I'm worse than a kid," Fargo said, and raised the bottle to his mouth. The swish of the whiskey was unnaturally loud. He was setting the bottle down when he looked along the bar toward a dark hall at the back and the short hairs at the nape of his neck prickled.

Someone was standing there looking back at him.

Fargo nearly jumped out of his chair. He couldn't make out much but he would swear that whoever it was wore some kind of frock or hood. "You there. Step out where I can see you."

The apparition retreated into the darkness.

"Damn it." Fargo was out of his chair like a shot, the Henry in his left hand. He raced to the hall and remembered to crouch so as not to be too good a target.

No sunlight penetrated, and it was mired in murk.

"I won't hurt you," Fargo thought to say. "I'm just passing through."

No one answered.

Fargo's temper flared. First the dogs and then the girl and now this. For a ghost town it wasn't short of the living. He edged forward, the Henry level.

Gradually his eyes adjusted to where he could make out

doors on both sides. He tried the door on the right. The latch rasped, and he pushed. The sunlight coming in a small glassless window revealed a room barren of everything save dust.

Fargo tried the other door. It opened into a larger room with a table and chairs. A private gambling room, he guessed. Strange that the owner had left furniture behind, but then, chairs and tables were cheap and maybe the owner didn't have room in his wagon. Fargo moved on. The end of the hall was black as pitch. He reached out and found another latch. A shove, and the door squeaked on noisy hinges. Chill air washed over him. Puzzled, he moved past the threshold only to find another barren room.

Fargo retraced his steps. He was sure he had seen someone. But then again, maybe it had been a trick of the shadows. He reclaimed his chair and tilted the bottle to his lips and looked out the window.

The Ovaro was gone.

The bottle crashed to the floor as Fargo heaved out of his chair and was past the batwing in long strides. He looked to one side and then the other. The street was deserted. His anger became fury. Taking a man's horse was a hanging offense. Or in his case, a shooting offense. He stepped to the hitch rail. In the dust, clear as could be, were the stallion's hoofprints, leading away.

Fargo was mystified. Why the hell hadn't the Ovaro whinnied? Most of the time, the stallion didn't like anyone touching it but him. There had been a few exceptions, notably female. The stallion was almost as fond of the fairer sex as he was. "You mangy cayuse," he muttered, not meaning a word of it.

Fargo bent. Along with the Ovaro's tracks were the footprints of the person who took him. They were smaller than a man's would be, and whoever made them was barefoot. That narrowed the suspects. He hurried down the street in the direction they took to a gap between what used to be a general store and a butcher shop.

"When I get hold of you, girl . . ." Fargo threw caution aside and broke into a run, his spurs jangling. He narrowly missed colliding with an upended barrel. Slowing as he came to the end, he warily poked his head out.

Beyond, a fringe of grass bordered dense forest. The tracks led into the trees.

Fargo's fury climbed. So did his worry. The girl might climb on and ride off, stranding him. He jogged in pursuit, praying for a glimpse. She couldn't have gone far, he told himself. A splash of white and black lent wings to his feet. He broke into a clearing and was overcome with relief.

The Ovaro was by itself. It was cropping grass, as unconcerned as if it were in a stable.

"You lunkhead." Fargo took another step, and stopped. Something was different about his saddle. There was dirt on it. Then he noticed that a clump of grass had been pulled out and the clod lay next to the Ovaro. "What the hell?"

He moved closer. The dirt was actually a word. It said simply, *"Go."*

Fargo stared at the clod, sorting it out in his head. The girl had taken his horse. She had led it out of town to get *him* out of town. Then she had pulled out the clod, moistened her finger, got dirt on it, and wrote on his saddle. That was a lot of trouble to go to just to get him to leave. And it raised a host of questions. Why didn't she just walk up to him and ask him? Why lure him away by taking the Ovaro? What was the business with sending her dogs after him and then they just up and vanished? In short, what the hell was going on?

Fargo wiped the dirt off. He stared through the trees at the ghost town and then at the stallion. The smart thing to do was exactly what the girl wanted. He had no interest in Kill Creek and didn't care about the man he saw in the saloon. Ride on, he told himself. Ride on, and forget this strangeness.

Gripping the reins, Fargo stepped into the stirrups. He reined around and rode back through the gap to the main street and along the street to the stable at the far end. The double doors were wide-open, one hanging by a hinge.

Fargo went in. The place smelled musty. He dismounted and proceeded to strip the Ovaro. His saddle went over a stall, his saddle blanket next to it. He led the stallion in and rubbed its neck. "Try to stay put this time."

To keep the dogs out he closed the double doors. He had to drag the one with the busted hinge.

Fargo returned to the saloon, his boots clomping on the boardwalk.

He didn't think the girl would take the Ovaro a second time. She must be wondering what he was up to just as he was wondering about her. He frowned when he saw the shattered bottle. He could use another drink.

Since it was early yet, Fargo decided to explore. He went from building to building looking for answers. Most places all he found was dust. The general store had been picked clean. Although the butcher was long since gone, the butcher shop had a lingering reek, as of meat gone bad.

In every place he went Fargo found footprints. Most were no more than smudges and scuffs but clearly someone had been roaming around Kill Creek for some time, doing God knew what.

The next building he came to was once a millinery. A blistered sign announced the finest in dresses and bonnets for ladies. He opened the door and was surprised when a bell tinkled. He was even more surprised at the carpet on the floor and the half dozen dresses that hung on a rack and the fact there was hardly any dust.

Fargo thought of the girl, of her homespun shirt and pants. If she was going to all this trouble to keep the millinery tidy and clean, why didn't she wear one of the dresses? In a room in the back was a cot in good condition. He tested it by sitting on it. As most cots did, the canvas tended to sag after a lot of use. The sag in this one told him it was used regularly. Again he thought of the redhead.

14

Fargo went back out. The sun had climbed considerably. He crossed the street and made for the creek and the diggings. He imagined the frenzy of the gold seekers as they dug and panned and dredged. All that was left was a rusty pan with a hole in the bottom and a discarded pick and shovel. He walked along looking for any sign of recent activity but found none. Apparently the creek had been panned out. Part of a bluff had been dug away revealing a vein of quartz that didn't have so much as a speck of gold.

Fargo glanced toward the ghost town and stiffened. A figure was at a window, watching him. It was the same one from the saloon, a big man in some sort of hood or cowl. The instant he spotted him, the man melted away.

Fargo pretended not to have noticed. He took his hat off and ran his hand through his hair and put his hat back on and ambled to the stable.

The Ovaro was still there, undisturbed. He slung his saddlebags over his shoulder and as he turned to go spied a lantern on a peg. He shook it, then opened it and sniffed. Whale oil. It should still work. He carried it out, closed the door, and walked to the saloon. From under his hat brim he peered at every window and studied every nook. He would swear unseen eyes were on him but he didn't spot anyone.

In the saloon he set the lantern on the table. Opening his saddlebags, he took out a bundle of pemmican. He turned the chair so he could see the street and the hallway at the back, both, and sat chewing and relaxing, the Henry at his elbow, his Colt loose in his holster.

Outside, the shadows lengthened.

Fargo hadn't been in a ghost town in a while. He had forgotten how eerie they could be. It was so quiet he could hear himself chew. He took out a deck of cards and played solitaire for a while. He checked under the bar for another bottle but luck didn't favor him a second time.

Along about five Fargo walked to the creek to slake his thirst. When he came back everything was as he had left it.

He sank into his chair and idly shuffled and reshuffled the cards, killing time, waiting for the redhead to make up her mind. If he knew human nature, and he flattered himself that he did, then sooner or later she would show herself.

Fargo went out on the boardwalk. The sun was low on the horizon, the sky ablaze with streaks of red, orange and yellow. Sunsets in the West had a habit of being spectacular. The few he saw when he ventured east of the Mississippi River were about as exciting as dishwater. He wondered why that was.

Fargo roamed the street, letting whoever was spying on him get a good look.

He took his time. Twilight was falling when he returned to the saloon and his chair. He had left the cards out and he put them in his saddlebags. The bundle of pemmican, too. To an onlooker it must have seemed as if he wasn't paying much attention to what was going on around him but his every sense was primed. When a shadowy form moved in the hall, he saw it right away. Leaning back, he casually lowered his hand until it brushed his Colt.

The shadow acquired substance, a hint of a shape, a suggestion of hair that fell past the shoulders.

Fargo went to reach for the lantern but decided not to light it. It might scare her off. He kept on pretending to look out the window and when she didn't step out of the hall he decided to seize the bull by the horns. "I know you're there."

She didn't respond.

"You might as well show yourself."

The figured emerged.

It was a woman, all right. Only she had black hair, not red, and as she came out she raised a revolver and pointed it at him.

"Move and I shoot you."

3

Fargo smiled and bobbed his chin at a chair a few yards away. "Have a seat. I wouldn't mind someone to talk to."

The woman cocked her head as if puzzled. She was young and pretty. Not as luscious as the redhead but she had a nice full figure. Her eyes were green. Her nose was a bit too wide, her lips a bit too thick, but Fargo was willing to bet those lips were deliciously soft, and what the hell did he care about noses? She came closer, the Smith and Wesson steady in her hand. She, too, wore a homespun shirt and pants and no shoes or boots. "Why aren't you scared?"

"If you were fixing to shoot me you could have done it from back in the hall." Fargo introduced himself. "What might your name be?"

The woman didn't answer. She walked to the chair and sat facing him with the revolver in her lap. Her green eyes narrowed and she studied him so intently, he almost laughed.

"Like what you see?"

"Why didn't you go?"

"I like what I see."

"I took your horse and wrote on your saddle but you came back. I was doing you a favor." She frowned and asked again, "Why didn't you go?"

"That was you? I thought it was a redheaded gal who runs with a pack of dogs."

"Maxine," the raven-haired lovely said. "She's my sister."

Fargo laced his fingers behind his head and raised a boot

to the table. "I ran into her not far from here and she set those dogs on me."

"She was probably trying to scare you off. Although with her there's never really any telling."

"What's that supposed to mean? And you still haven't told me who you are."

"My name is Serilda. That's all you need to know. I say too much, my pa will be mad at me." Serilda bit her lower lip and glanced back at the hall and then out at the street. "You really should go before he comes back or before they show up."

"They who?"

"You don't want to get mixed up in this. You really don't." Serilda lowered her voice and said with undeniable sincerity, "I don't want anything to happen to you, is all."

"What do you care?" Fargo bluntly asked. "I'm a stranger."

"You're a human being and I don't want you harmed." Serilda leaned forward. "Please. Get on your horse and skedaddle. Now. Right this minute. They could show up anytime and then it will be too late."

"There you go again, talking in riddles." Fargo smiled to lessen the sting. "Besides, now that I've met you, maybe I don't want to leave." He roved his gaze from her black curls to her dirty bare feet and back again.

"Aren't you the brazen one? You just come out and tell a woman, is that right?"

"Life is too short to beat around the bush." Fargo had an idea. "What do you say to rustling up some grub and the two of us getting better acquainted?"

"You want me to cook you a meal?"

"I'll do the cooking," Fargo offered. He certainly did enough of it on the trail, and truth to tell, was better at it than most. "You supply the food." All he had in his saddlebags was the pemmican. He had been living off the land as he went.

"I couldn't," Serilda said. "Pa would cane me. Maxine would have a fit. Then there are those others."

"Riddles, riddles, riddles."

Serilda came out of the chair and over to him and placed her hand on his arm. "Please. This isn't a game. It's worth your life if you stay. I mean that with all my heart."

Fargo could see that she was serious. "Don't fret none about me. I can take care of myself."

Serilda stepped back and scowled. "Men. Trying to talk sense into them is like trying to talk sense into tree stumps."

"We have our uses," Fargo said with a smirk.

"Is that all you ever think of?"

Fargo shrugged. "When I'm not playing cards or drinking or on the trail. What else is there?"

"There's a lot more to life than *that*. There is money and nice clothes and a fine house to live in." Serilda's eyes glowed with longing. "I would give anything to have enough money to buy all the nice things I want. To get a new dress. And shoes. And to live in a house with a bed and a kitchen and everything."

"Is that your cot in the dress shop?"

Serilda gave a start. "You've been there? I wouldn't go anywhere near there again if I were you."

"It's just a cot."

"Pa won't take kindly to you nosing around. He doesn't cotton to strangers. He thinks they are . . ." Serilda stopped and puckered those thick lips of hers. "Why are you wasting time like this? *Please* go. I don't want you on my conscience. There are too many already."

"Riddles," Fargo said again.

Serilda went to the window and looked up the street. "God, it's almost dark. They'll be here soon. He said by sundown."

"Who did?"

Serilda turned. "Would you stick your head in a bear trap?

19

Or poke a riled rattler? No one would. But that's exactly what you're doing and you don't even know it."

"I know I like your body."

"You never stop, do you?!" Serilda suddenly went rigid and spun. "Wait. Did you hear something? A wagon, maybe?"

"No." Fargo hadn't heard a thing.

"I thought I did." Serilda pressed her face to the cracked pane and then jerked back and went past the table toward the back. She stopped halfway there. "I'll try one last time. Are you leaving or not?"

"Not," Fargo said.

"Then I wish you the best."

Fargo was out of his chair. "Wait," he called out. He ran to the hall but couldn't see her. "Where did you get to?" When she didn't answer he went to each of the doors and opened them. To his consternation she wasn't in any of the rooms. She had vanished.

Fargo hurried to the table. He raised the glass on the lantern so he could light the wick and opened his saddlebags to rummage for a box of Bryant and May matches a farmer's wife had given him.

From down the street came a loud noise, a gigantic thud as if something heavy had fallen over.

Fargo scooped up the Henry and ran out. The sun was gone and a few stars sparkled overhead. Night was crawling over Kill Creek. The buildings were vague shapes. He ran toward the stable and alarm spiked him when he saw that the door that had been hanging by one hinge had torn loose and lay on the ground. He ran inside and over to the stall and was elated to find the Ovaro still there. Patting it, he said, "I thought maybe someone had taken you again."

The stallion's head was up and its ear pricked and it was staring at a corner of the stable to the right of the doors.

Fargo looked but saw nothing. The corner was as black as the bottom of a well. He had learned, though, to trust the stallion's senses. Raising the Henry to his shoulder, he said, "Show yourself."

The wind fanned the dust. Otherwise, nothing stirred.

Fargo moved toward the corner. He had taken only a couple of steps when a patch of black exploded into motion. In a blur a large shape rushed to the door and out into the night. It was the figure from the saloon, the one wearing some sort of brown frock or robe with a hood that covered their head and most of their face.

"Hold on." Fargo gave chase. He didn't fire. The figure's hands were empty and whoever it was hadn't attacked him. "I just want to talk."

The man sped down the street with a speed Fargo was hard-pressed to match. Suddenly the figure ducked into the gap between the general store and the butcher's. Fargo wasn't more than twenty feet behind him, yet when he came to the gap, no one was there.

It was impossible. The man hadn't had time to reach the other end. Fargo scratched his beard in bewilderment. First the figure and then Serilda had disappeared in the saloon, and now this. There had to be an explanation and he would find out what it was. He wheeled and stalked back. The wick proved stubborn. He succeeded in lighting it and raised the lantern and turned to go to the back hall—and drew up short.

Maxine was at the bar. She was leaning back, propped on her elbows, her beauty breathtaking in the lantern's glow. Any man would give anything to be with a woman like her. She regarded him coldly and said with an edge of flint, "Just what in hell are you doing here, mister?"

"I could ask you the same question."

"You only think you can. Set that rifle on the table and don't you dare try to touch that six-gun."

"You're threatening me?"

"I'm warning you." Maxine gestured toward the opposite side of the saloon.

Fargo turned and raised the lantern higher so that its glow

splashed the entire room and there they were, the four mastiffs, lying near the far wall. One of the beasts growled. The others stared expectantly at their mistress, awaiting her command.

"You can't shoot them all before they get to you and those that do will rip you to pieces."

"Is that why you sent them after me earlier today?"

"The rifle," Maxine said. "Put it on the table."

Fargo did as she wanted, for now. She might be right about him not being able to drop all four before they reached him and it would take only one to inflict a serious if not fatal wound. He set the Henry down and the lantern next to it, and then leaned against the table with his arms folded across his chest. "All right. We'll do this your way."

"Smart man." Maxine's lips quirked. "As for sending them after you, I was trying to scare you off. I didn't tell them to attack, just to chase. They're well trained."

"I believe you."

"But you were too dumb to take the hint. Is it that you're naturally stupid or just that you're male?"

"Your sister tried to talk me into leaving, too," Fargo mentioned. "What do you have against strangers?"

"Damn her," Maxine said. "I knew she had snuck up here. I told her not to. I said if we left you be, you'd see there wasn't anything here for you and go on your way. But no. She was worried for you."

"That was nice of her."

"Nice, hell. She's too kindhearted for her own good. She has to learn to do what's best for us whether she likes it or not." Maxine gave an angry toss of her red mane. "Enough about Serilda. I'm not her so I won't ask you nice to leave Kill Creek. I am *telling* you to get the hell out."

"I don't like being bossed around."

"I don't blame you. I don't either. But it's for your own good. If you stay the night you'll wind up like the others."

"What others?" Fargo probed.

Maxine bowed her head and a tinge of sadness marked her lovely features.

"There have been half a dozen or so. They wander in and they think to stay the night, and that's what always does it. By morning they are dead and there's nothing my sister or me can do."

"How do they die?"

"They die so quick they don't see it coming. They never stand a prayer. You won't be any different."

Fargo got to the pertinent point. "Who does the killing? That joker in the hood?"

"You've seen Pa, then?"

"Two times."

"And you're still breathing? He must figure you're not planning to stay, or we wouldn't be having this little talk. You'd be dead by now. The only other one he didn't kill was because I took a fancy . . ." Maxine stopped.

"Go on."

Maxine straightened and crossed the saloon to her dogs. Squatting, she petted two of them and said over her shoulder, "These are the best friends I have in the whole wide world. I don't want them hurt but I will by God have them kill you if you don't do as I say."

"Damn it. The least you could do is tell me what this is all about."

Maxine swiveled. "No, I can't. It's none of your business, for one thing. And it's personal, for another." She rose. "I'll give you half an hour to be on your way. If you're still here after that, then it will be my dogs or it will be him but either way you won't live to see the dawn."

Fargo looked at the mastiffs.

"Don't even think it. I just told you, they're my friends. You shoot them, I'll shoot you."

Fargo believed she would, too.

"Remember. Half an hour." Maxine strode to the single batwing. "Stay a minute longer and you can kiss this life good-bye."

"The only thing I want to kiss around here is you," Fargo said. Which wasn't entirely true. There was Serilda.

Maxine snorted. "Listen to you. Do you reckon I must be starved for it, living so far from everywhere? If you only knew." On that enigmatic note she pushed on the batwing. "Heel," she said to the mastiffs, and went out. Instantly, the four dogs rose and filed from the saloon, each glancing at Fargo as it went by. The one that had growled before growled again.

"Hell," Skye Fargo said.

4

Fargo decided it just wasn't worth it. The two women were enough to make any man's mouth water but a tumble on a cot wasn't worth being torn to bits or shot. It galled him, though, being told to leave, or else.

Gathering up the Henry and the lantern, he headed for the stable. Night gripped the Sierra Nevadas. From out of the northwest blew a brisk wind that brought with it the howls of wolves. To the east coyotes yipped. The roar of a grizzly was added proof that the meat-eaters were abroad. To most people they were fearsome sounds that sent shivers down many a spine. To him it was the music of the wild.

Fargo stepped over the fallen door and was about to enter when from out of the night came a loud racket: the pounding of hooves and the rattling of wheels and a man's gruff voice bellowing a command. Points of light appeared.

Someone was coming up the road from the west.

Fargo ducked into the stable. Given all that had happened he wasn't taking any chances. He blew out the lantern and hung it on a peg and then crouched next to the doorway.

The points of light grew bigger and the racket swelled and into view swept a stagecoach flanked by half a dozen riders. Three held lanterns. They were moving faster than a stage normally would at night but with the lanterns it was easy for the driver to control the team. He cracked his whip and bellowed again.

Fargo was puzzled. So far as he knew, the Amador Stage Line was the only one operating in northern California. But it made no sense for them to send a stage to a ghost town. It couldn't be a normal run. And why did the stage appear to have an armed escort? He wasn't given time to ponder. The stage came clattering into Kill Creek and the lead rider called out for it to stop as it neared the stable.

The driver pulled back and shouted, "Whoa, there. Whoa."

Fargo turned. He'd rather not make his presence known but there was nowhere to hide. The stable didn't have a hay-loft and the dark corners wouldn't stay dark if the men with the lanterns came in. He ran to the Ovaro's stall and slipped in. "Easy, boy." Moving to the back, he hunkered.

From outside came the blowing of the team and the stamping of a hoof or two, and voices.

Spurs jingled and light bathed the stable.

Fargo peered through cracks between the boards.

A burly man with a six-shooter on either hip and wearing a broad-brimmed hat and a slicker had opened the other door and was holding a lantern over his head. Stubble peppered his chin and he had a scar on his left cheek. Everything about him said hardcase as plainly as if he wore a sign on his chest. "What the hell?" he exclaimed. "There's a horse in here, Landreth."

Another man entered. This one was different. His clothes were the latest city fashion, including an expensive coat and bowler and knee-high black boots. He carried a cane. "It's *Mr.* Landreth to you, Mr. Moon. How many times must I remind you?"

The two-gun man scowled and said, "The airs you put on. I will only abide so much. Keep that in mind."

"We have an agreement," Landreth said stiffly. He moved past the other and came close to the stall. The Ovaro raised its head but didn't whinny or spook.

"A fine animal, this."

26

"It means someone else is here. Someone who shouldn't be."

"You figured that out, did you?" Landreth said. "I must say, your keen intellect continues to impress me."

"Dig yourself deeper," Moon replied.

"Whoever it is, he's only one man and there are seven of us. We have nothing to fear."

"How do you know it's a him?"

"Be sensible. Do women travel alone through these mountains? I think not. No, it's some mountain man or a prospector or perhaps a wandering cowpoke. We must be sure to send him on his way as soon as we find him." Landreth went to the door. "I'll inform James."

"Why don't you call him Jim? That's what most folks would do."

"He prefers James and he's my friend." Landreth strolled out.

Moon hung his lantern on a peg near the one Fargo had used. He started to turn, glanced at the other lantern, and touched it. Jerking his fingers back, he spun, his hands swooping to his twin Remingtons. He scanned the stable suspiciously and started down the center aisle.

Another man entered. This one was tall and lanky and like Moon wore a slicker but only one revolver. He was leading a bay and when he saw Moon with his hands on his Remingtons he said, "Something the matter?"

Moon nodded at the Ovaro. "Take a gander."

"Where the hell did that come from? We didn't count on anybody else being here."

"It doesn't change a thing, Conklin. We'll do what we have to, and if it comes to it, he'll be just one more to buck out in gore."

Conklin brought the bay over to the stalls. Instead of stripping the saddle, he tied the bay to a post.

Fargo put his eye to the crack. Thanks to the lanterns he

27

could see that three other men in slickers were taking the team out of harness. The driver stayed up on the seat. Landreth was at the coach, talking in low tones to someone inside. Soon the three men brought the horses in and placed them in stalls. Then, assisted by Moon and Conklin, the men in slickers grabbed hold of the tongue and with a lot of grunting and heaving, wheeled the stagecoach into the stable, hind end foremost.

Landreth walked beside it and didn't offer to help.

The driver caught Fargo's interest. A grizzled veteran of his trade with gray in his hair, he wore buckskins and a short-brimmed brown hat. He also had a gun belt around his waist but the holster was empty. As the stage came to a stop, he leaned over the side and said to Landreth, "I hope you rot in hell, you son of a bitch."

The dandy glanced up sharply. He gave his cane a twirl and said curtly, "For a gent who has served his purpose, you are awful free with your tongue, old man."

"Listen to you. You even talk like a weak sister."

"Have a care, Hornsby. You'll provoke me one too many times and it will be the death of you."

"I'm plumb scared to death, boy."

Landreth started to raise his cane but just then the stage door opened and another man emerged. Strikingly handsome, he was about Landreth's age, and like Landreth, fancied fine clothes. He wore a tailored blue coat and white pants with blue stripes. His hat made Fargo think of a pheasant about to take flight. It had a high crown with feathers on one side and the front was decorated with pearls. A Cossack hat, Fargo thought they called it.

"Enough, you two. This petty bickering will stop. Do you hear me?" He gazed up at Hornsby. "I especially don't want any more trouble from you."

"You damned whippersnapper. I would pistol-whip you if your hired vermin hadn't taken my pistol."

Landreth said, "We're making a mistake, James. This old

coot can identify us. Why not do as Moon wants? One less worry."

"No," James said, and smoothed his blue coat. "We'll do this my way. No lives are to be taken unless I say they are."

"As you wish."

Moon and Conklin and the other men in slickers had been listening, and Moon said to James, "How in hell a man like you came up with a notion like this is beyond me."

"Necessity, Mr. Moon, is the midwife of many an exigency."

"A what?"

"More simply put: we do what we have to."

"Why didn't you say that, then? You and your big words. Half the time I have no idea what the hell you're talking about."

James adjusted his Cossack hat. "I do wish you would refrain from swearing in their presence. I grant that you aren't a gentleman but you could try to behave like one, as much as I am paying you."

Moon's mouth curled as if he had sucked on a bitter lemon.

"Paying us? Mister, we ain't seen a cent yet. This plan of yours better damn well work or there will be hell to pay."

"It will, I assure you."

"Promises won't fill our pokes," Moon informed him.

Landreth ran a finger along his pencil-thin mustache. "James never makes a promise he can't keep. He said you will receive ten thousand dollars, and you will."

"Ten thousand *each*," Moon said.

"Yes, yes," James responded as if irritated. "For a grand total of fifty thousand. A trifle, really."

"Is it, now." Moon glanced at Conklin and the lanky gun shark grinned.

"Which reminds me. You've never said exactly how much you hope to get."

"All you need know is what I've already told you." James

faced the stagecoach and held out a hand. "I'm sorry, my dears, for neglecting you. Permit me to help you."

A face appeared, a female face, framed by a bonnet. The woman who lowered a dainty foot to step down had every curl of her brown hair in place and wore a dress that most women couldn't afford if they saved every dollar for a year. She had a pointed chin and a nose that came to a sharp tip and lips so thin they were hardly lips at all. "Thank you, James," she said in a voice as thin as her lips. "A perfect gentleman, as always."

"Would you expect less of me, Esther?"

Esther made a show of smoothing her dress while saying, "If I did I wouldn't be here."

James turned to the open door of the stagecoach. "And how about you, my dear? Surely you don't intend to sit in there all night?"

Another female face appeared. This one was much more appealing. Yellow hair and blue eyes lent an angelic aspect. Her clothes were not as costly as Esther's but they still set her back a pretty penny. Instead of taking James's proffered hand, she stepped down herself. "It will take longer than one night and you know it."

"True, Gretchen," James responded. "Up to ten days if all goes well, longer if there are delays."

"I hope they refuse," Gretchen said.

James and Landreth both laughed and James said, "The Mindels refuse to save their precious pride and joy? I think not. In ten days time I'll have enough money to live comfortably for the rest of my life."

From his hiding place Fargo was the only one who saw Moon and Conklin once again swap looks.

"You're despicable," Gretchen said.

Esther stopped fussing with her clothes and smacked her small hand against her thin leg. "That's enough. Do you hear me? I put up with you sulking the whole way here but it must stop."

"Being abducted will do that."

"There you go again." Esther shook her head. "I honestly expected better of you. You don't see me pouting and acting immature."

Moon stuck his thumbs in his gun belt and sauntered over. They didn't notice until he poked James with a finger. "Enough of this gab. My men and me have been in the saddle since before dawn and we're tuckered out. We need to find a place to sleep."

"The rudeness," Landreth said.

James motioned. "No, he has a point. It's been a long day for all of us. I say we find rooms for the ladies and post a guard and then the rest of us will turn in."

"A guard?" Gretchen repeated.

"It's for your own good, really. Ghost towns are not always empty." James pointed at the Ovaro. "Case in point."

"Who does that belong to?" Esther asked.

"We have no idea. Mr. Moon, finding out will be your job. Have two of your men search the town while the rest carry our bags."

Moon turned to Conklin. "You heard the man. Take Shorty with you. Nose into every cranny. Whoever it is was bound to have heard the stage. Most folks would be curious but no one has shown up. That tells me he's hiding."

"He's as good as caught," Conklin predicted. He and the shortest of them left the stable.

"What about me?" Hornsby asked.

James and Landreth had taken the arms of the ladies and were to escort them out. Gretchen, Fargo noticed, let Landreth take hers reluctantly.

"My word. I forgot all about you," James said. "I leave it up to you. Would you like to find a room or stay with your stage?"

"That's a stupid question if ever I heard one," the cantankerous driver replied.

"No need to be insulting."

"Sonny, what do you use for brains? You had your monkeys stop my stage at gunpoint. Then you made me drive twelve hours over a road barely fit for a Concord. And now, if I heard rightly, you said I'll be stuck here for ten days or more. I'd say being rude is letting you off easy."

Moon had lowered his hands to his holsters. "Did you just call me an ape, you old goat?"

"I called you a monkey but ape will do. So will bastard, son of a bitch, no account, buzzard and polecat. Take your pick."

James said, "I'll have none of that. Not unless you want to be tied up and gagged until the ten days are up."

"I don't like being called names," Moon declared. "I never have and I never will."

"Ignore the old goat," James said.

"I'd like to see the peckerwood try," Hornsby taunted.

Moon's jaw muscles twitched. "Some folks don't have no more sense than to talk themselves into an early grave."

The Remingtons flashed and boomed.

5

There was nothing Fargo could do. It happened too fast. Moon was quick on the draw, one of the quickest Fargo ever saw. Even if Hornsby had been armed he wouldn't have stood a prayer.

Moon fired from the hip. He didn't take aim. As impressive as his speed was his accuracy. Both shots cored the driver's head, blowing out the back of his skull and sending Hornsby toppling from the seat to the ground.

The woman called Gretchen put a hand to her throat and turned away from the grisly sight. The woman called Esther, strangely enough, laughed.

"Here now!" James said. Squatting next to the body, he uselessly felt for a pulse. "That was uncalled for, Mr. Moon."

"I won't be called names."

"I told you no killing unless it was absolutely necessary. You remember that, don't you?"

"Mister, there ain't enough room in my noggin for all the words you use." Moon still held his Remingtons. He swiveled toward Landreth and growled, "How about you, dandy man? You have anything to say?"

Landreth wasn't cowed. He pointed his cane at Moon, and glared. "Don't threaten me, you ignoramus. Shoot me and you won't get a dollar. You'll have gone to all this trouble for nothing."

"It might be worth it," Moon said.

James moved between them. "I won't have any of this, either. We must work together, not against one another. Mr. Moon, put those away, if you please."

"Sure, city boy." Moon twirled the Remingtons into their holsters and hooked his thumbs in his gun belt. "Happy now?"

"Very much so, yes," James said. He stared at the dead stage driver. "The authorities will charge you with murder over this. You'll have to bury the body."

"How will the law know I did it unless someone tells them?" Moon rejoined.

"Whether they do or they don't isn't the point. I don't like that you have unwittingly given them more cause to hunt us down."

"Unwitting—what? Are you saying I'm stupid?"

"Quit putting words in my mouth." James turned to him. "You agreed to my terms when I hired you and one of those terms was no killing."

"You keep saying that. Now let me remind you." Moon grated his next words through clenched lips. "Insult me and die."

"This is getting us nowhere. We need to cooperate if we are to get through this safely. I'm bound for Europe, afterward, and you"—James paused—"What *will* you do with your share of the money?"

"What I always do with money. Drink, gamble and buy me some whores. A whole lot of whores."

"How vulgar," Esther remarked.

"Another damn insult," Moon said.

"Enough." James took Esther's arm. "Come, my dear. We'll see about rooms for the two of you. For however long we are here, I'll do all in my power to make your stay as comfortable as humanly possible."

Landreth reached for Gretchen but she pulled her arm free. "I can walk without your help, thank you very much."

Esther tittered. "Must you make such a fuss? Try to get along. It will make our stay easier to bear."

"Speak for yourself."

James guided Esther around a spreading pool of blood. "Come on. Mr. Moon, don't forget the firewood. Roy, bring a lantern, if you would. I'm tired and need rest."

Landreth took a lantern from one of Moon's men and the two city men and the ladies departed.

From his hiding place Fargo saw Moon scowl and then heard him say, "High and mighty city folk. I don't like any of them even a little bit."

One of the remaining men in slickers said, "They sure are uppity."

"It comes from being rich, Tucker," Moon said. "They reckon they should be treated special for being born with silver spoons in their mouths."

"I'd like to have a silver spoon in mine," Tucker said. "I could sell it for drinking money."

Moon looked at him and grinned. "That's why I keep you around. We think alike."

"Want Beck and me to see to the burying?"

"Bury, hell. Why bother?" Moon went over and kicked Hornsby's mortal remains. "Drag his carcass off into the woods and cover it with a few leaves and branches."

"The coyotes and buzzards are bound to get to it."

"So? Critters have to eat the same as the rest of us." Moon started for the doors. "Gather some firewood while you're at it. We might as well do our part until the money gets here."

Tucker bent and gripped one of Hornsby's arms. Beck was holding a lantern and used his free hand to grab the other. Together they hauled the body out, leaving a scarlet trail in their wake.

The stable plunged into darkness.

Fargo stayed where he was, pondering. Apparently the two women had been abducted. For ransom, from the sound of things. He remembered Serilda had made a remark about expecting someone to show up, and he wondered if this was what she meant.

Fargo had a decision to make. He could saddle the Ovaro and sneak off and leave this whole mess for the law to clean up. That was the smart thing to do. These people meant nothing to him. He didn't know Esther or Gretchen. He barely knew Serilda and Maxine.

Whatever they were up to was none of his concern.

Warily, Fargo rose and stepped to the front of the stall. His saddle and saddle blanket were in easy reach. He didn't need light to throw them on the stallion. He had done it so many times, he could do it blindfolded.

Fargo hesitated. He thought of the look on Gretchen's face when Hornsby was shot. He thought of Maxine and her perfect face and body and Serilda with her black curls and full lips, and he said quietly to himself, "Damn me for a fool."

Hunkering, Fargo removed his spurs. He went to put them in his saddlebags and realized he had left the saddlebags in the saloon.

Annoyed at his carelessness, he placed his spurs in a corner of the stall where they were less likely to be noticed. Then he crept to the open doors and peered out.

Down the street Conklin and Shorty were going from building to building, searching. James and Landreth and the ladies had stopped in front of the millinery and were talking. Moon was ambling toward them. No one was looking toward the stable.

Staying close to the wall, Fargo eased out. He came to the corner and heard low voices and risked a peek.

Tucker and Beck were dragging the body into the forest.

"Damn, this old coot is heavy," the latter complained.

"We won't take him far," Tucker said. "Just so the smell won't bother us when he gets ripe."

Fargo cat-footed on. He stayed in the darkest patches and stopped whenever anyone down the street glanced in his direction. He made it to the saloon undetected and slipped under the batwing and over to the table where he had left his saddlebags.

They weren't there.

Fargo ran his hands over the top of the table to be sure, and swore. He didn't think the newcomers were to blame. That left Maxine or Serilda or their pa.

He crossed to the hallway. It was so dark he had to feel his way. He checked the room on the right and the room on the left. Both were empty. That left the room at the end. It was open a few inches and as he came up he felt another puff of cool air. Pushing, he entered and went from wall to wall, lightly knocking every few feet. He wanted to pound harder but they'd hear out in the street.

Fargo was convinced there must be a secret way in and out. It was the only explanation for how Serilda and her father had disappeared. But the walls seemed solid. He squatted and was about to check the floor when he heard voices from out at the front.

Rising, Fargo hurried out. He'd gone only a few steps when the saloon was splashed by the rosy glow of lantern light. Boots thumped, and someone laughed. Wheeling, he retreated into the back room and closed the door nearly all the way.

". . . will do as good as anywhere. Have them fetch their bedrolls."

Fargo recognized Moon's voice. It was Conklin who answered.

"I'll get yours and mine."

"Wait a minute. I don't savvy how you didn't find anyone."

"Me either. Shorty and me went through every building."

"That horse in the stable didn't put itself there."

"Maybe it belongs to the freak or his girls."

"I doubt they even own a horse," Moon said. "Him and his moles don't have any need for one."

Fargo wondered what they were talking about. Conklin's next remark provided a clue.

"They sure are the prettiest moles I ever did see. I wouldn't say no to a poke with either one. No offense."

"That's all you ever think of. Poking."

"A man takes them where he can get them," Conklin said.

"Don't try with them."

"I wouldn't think of it. Those dogs give me a scare. They can rip a man's throat without half trying."

"Maxine better keep them out of sight," Moon said. "I don't want it spoiled."

"Only you would think of something like this," Conklin said by way of praise. "You're the cleverest cuss I ever met."

"A chance like this doesn't come along but once in a man's life, if that. I'd be a fool to let it slip through my fingers."

"I can't wait to see the look on their faces."

"Just don't give it away before the riders get here. Remind the others to keep their mouths shut. I'll kill the man who spoils it."

"We want it as much as you do."

"All my life I've hoped for a break like this." A chair scraped, and then Moon said, "Collect everybody. I want to go over it again so they have it clear in their heads."

"We've talked it to death," Conklin said. "We'll play along just like you told us."

"Collect them, I said."

"Right away." Boots thudded and the saloon became quiet. Fargo opened the door another few inches and saw Moon at the table, boots propped up, staring out the window. A lantern was beside him.

Fargo was tired of the cat and mouse. Since he couldn't find any other way out, he either had to stay hid until Moon and his friends left or show himself.

To hell with it, he thought. Just as he came to the main room, a board creaked under his boot.

Moon came out of the chair lightning swift. His hands swooped to his Remingtons but he didn't draw. He stared hard at Fargo and then demanded, "Who the hell are you?"

"You first."

Moon looked him up and down. "When I ask a question I expect it to be answered."

Fargo ignored him and walked to the batwing. He spied Conklin but no one else. "How many of you are there?"

Moon stepped away from the table, his hands close to his holsters. "Mister, I'd damn well look at me when I'm talking to you."

Fargo faced him. "You're welcome to try."

Moon was still studying him. His dark eyes narrowed and his fingers twitched. "Folks say I'm awful quick."

"Folks say the same about me."

"I ain't never been beat."

"Makes two of us." Fargo was amused. They were like two bulls pawing at the ground. Only he doubted Moon would try him then and there. If Moon was half as clever as Conklin claimed, Moon would want to take his measure before resorting to hot lead.

Some of the tension drained from Moon's stance. He raised a hand and rubbed his chin. "All I want to know is who you are and what you're doing here."

Fargo leaned against the jamb. "I'm passing through on my way to San Francisco. I was sleeping in the back and voices woke me up."

"That pinto in the stable must be yours."

"It's not a pinto but he's mine and he better be there when I go for him," Fargo said.

"Rest easy. I'm no rustler." Moon leaned against the table. "They call me Moon on account of when I was younger I used to get drunk a lot and howl at it. What do they call you?"

"Fargo."

Moon hooked his thumbs in his gun belt. "It seems to me I've heard that name somewhere."

"Wells Fargo, maybe."

"No. Somewhere else. Some names you don't forget and that's one of them. Help me out."

Fargo shrugged and said, "It's not as if I'm famous."

"You're sure not a gold hound. Your clothes are too clean and you don't smell of dirt. What is it you do, exactly?"

"You're too nosy," Fargo said.

"I'm only asking. And I did it nice and polite."

Fargo decided it wouldn't matter. "I scout some. I guide wagon trains. I play cards."

"So you're a gambling man, are you? How about—" Moon stopped and his head snapped up.

Fargo heard it, too.

From down the street came a piercing scream.

6

Fargo was outside first. Down the street James and Landreth burst from the general store and raced toward the millinery. Conklin and Shorty came running from the far end.

Moon shoved the batwing wide. He glanced over when Fargo fell into step beside him. "I don't recollect asking you to tag along."

"A female screams like that, it means trouble."

"This female ain't none of your concern. She's with us. We'll take care of her."

Fargo kept running.

"You don't listen worth a damn."

"I bet folks say the same about you."

Moon actually laughed. "I'm beginning to like you, Fargo, and I can't have that. Not when I might have to kill you."

Conklin and Shorty were outside the millinery, and Conklin was mad. "That jackass wouldn't let us go in," he declared as Moon came up. "He said the ladies might not be decent."

"Stay here."

Moon opened the door, Fargo a step behind them. An old lamp spilled light over an empty rack that once held dresses and a small counter where the proprietor had sold them. The living quarters were at the back.

Esther and Gretchen were wearing robes. Gretchen's was wool and covered her from neck to ankle but Esther's was the sheerest silk and hid nothing. She didn't seem to care. She clung to James and gripped his jacket.

". . . seen the thing! It was hideous. I'm sorry I screamed but I couldn't help myself."

Landreth heard the clomp of Moon's boots and spun. "What the devil are you doing in here? Go back out this instant." He started to raise his cane.

"I wouldn't unless you're partial to lead," Moon warned. "What was that yell all about?"

James had an arm around Esther. "Miss Mindel was getting ready to retire and saw someone staring in the window at them."

"It was hideous," Esther repeated. "A monster. Like something out of a nightmare. I only caught a glimpse but it scared me half to death."

"Did you see it?" James asked Gretchen, who shook her head. He turned to Landreth. "Oversee a search. Moon and his men will help. We were told this town was empty but there's that horse in the stable and now this. Maybe the person Esther saw owns it."

"That would be me." Fargo stepped from behind Moon.

James and the others looked at him, and Landreth said, "What the deuce? Who are you and what are you doing here?"

"Shouldn't you be looking for a monster?" Fargo rejoined.

"He's right," James said. "Get out there and see what you can find. We'll talk to him later."

Landreth muttered and left with Moon while James ushered Esther toward the back. That left Fargo alone with Gretchen. Smiling, he offered his hand and said who he was.

She acted surprised by the gesture. Tentatively shaking, she said, "Gretchen Worth."

"What's a lovely lady like you doing in a ghost town in the middle of the night?" Fargo feigned ignorance.

Gretchen hesitated. Finally she said, "It's complicated."

"What isn't these days?" Fargo looked her up and down and said, "I like how you fill out that robe."

"I beg your pardon?"

"You have a nice body."

Now it was Gretchen who looked him up and down. "I don't know whether to laugh or slap you."

"Either will do. If you want I can sneak back later and we can go for a walk in the moonlight."

"I hardly know you, sir."

"An hour under the moon with me and you'll know all you need to."

Gretchen started to laugh but caught herself. "Really, now. You're impossible. You can't just walk up to a lady and ask her to do what you're asking me to do. It isn't done."

"It's done all the time. Or didn't your ma ever tell you where babies come from?"

"I am beginning to think you're serious."

"I am." Fargo gave her his best smile and lightly touched her hand. "I'll be out back in an hour."

"You presume too much," Gretchen said stiffly. "I can't think of any reason why I would."

"I can." Fargo lowered his voice. "You need a friend and I'm the only one you can trust."

"Trust a total stranger? Don't be absurd."

Fargo decided to confide in her. "I was in the stable. I overheard a lot and saw them kill the stage driver. I can get you and your friend out of here if you want. Think about it and meet me in an hour."

Gretchen didn't say anything and just then James came out of the back and over to Fargo. He offered his hand.

"James Harker. I didn't catch your name, sir."

Once more Fargo introduced himself.

"I'm going to help in the search for whoever was staring in at the women. Would you care to join me?"

Fargo shrugged. "Why not?" He glanced at Gretchen as he went out. She gazed thoughtfully after him, her lovely lips pursed.

The other men were running up and down the street and poking their heads into doors.

"No one here!"

"The butcher shop is empty!"

"So is the store!"

James entered a frame house shrouded in gloom and stopped past the threshold. "Is anyone here?"

Fargo wondered if he really expected someone to answer. "Mind if I ask what you and your friends are doing here?"

"We're on an outing," the dandy glibly answered. "An excursion, you might call it. We plan to stay here a few days and wander about. For the fun of it, you understand."

"Having fun so far?"

James frowned and hastened to a cabin. The door was on the ground and there was no glass in the window. Sticking his head in, he shouted, "Is anyone in here? I'd like to talk to you."

"I doubt the monster will answer."

"There's no such thing. Esther is high-strung. She saw someone staring in and didn't get a good look at him and her imagination took over." James went on to a shack in severe disrepair. "I'm mainly doing this to humor her." He suddenly stopped. "Say, I just had a thought. This person wouldn't happen to be with you, would he?"

"Afraid not."

They were almost to the shack when a small shape bolted out of high weeds.

James leaped back, his hand sweeping under his jacket. "Did you see that? It almost attacked me. What was it?"

"Folks hereabouts call them rabbits."

"That's all it was? I didn't get a good look. It was moving too fast."

"You scared it."

"Then we're even. It scared me."

"They do have big teeth," Fargo said dryly.

"I'm sorry if I appear foolish. I'm under a bit of a strain." He took a breath and composed himself and took a step toward the shack but stopped and said, "This is pointless, isn't it?"

"I'd say so. Whoever peeked in that window has had

plenty of time to hide." Fargo had an idea who it was but he kept it to himself.

"Who can it have been?" James asked, more to himself. "Mr. Moon assured us this town was abandoned and desolate. It seemed perfect for our plans."

"What plans are they?"

James turned and brushed past Fargo toward the street. "I thank you for your help. Now if you'll excuse me, I must gather the members of my party and get a few things settled."

Fargo would like to overhear what was said. He figured they'd meet either at the stable or the saloon. To avoid being seen, he jogged around to the rear of the shack and then along the back of the buildings. Some had back doors, some didn't. He was passing the back door to the general store, which was wide open, when a voice he recognized whispered, "Hold up."

Out stepped Serilda, the Smith and Wesson in her hand. "I want to ask you something."

"I'll answer if you stop pointing that thing at me."

"A girl has to watch out for herself," Serilda said, but she lowered it.

"What was all the ruckus about?"

"A monster is going around peeking into windows," Fargo joked, and was puzzled by her reaction.

Uttering a gasp of alarm, she blurted, "I knew he wouldn't do as they want. It was too much to ask."

"Knew who wouldn't?"

"It will be just like before. Blood will be spilled. A whole lot of blood. And there's nothing I can do to stop it. God help me, there isn't."

"It would help if you made more sense."

Serilda jerked the Smith and Wesson up and pointed it at his middle. "You're leaving Kill Creek."

"When I'm ready," Fargo said.

"No. You're lighting a shuck *now*. I'm marching you to the stable. You're to saddle your horse and go, and you can thank your lucky stars I'm being so considerate."

"Lady, as far as I'm concerned, you're plumb loco." Fargo was exaggerating but he wanted to rile her. He succeeded.

Serilda took a step. "Damn it. I'm doing this for your own good. You've blundered into something that could get you killed and I don't want more innocent blood on my hands."

"If I refuse?"

The click of the Smith and Wesson's hammer was ominously loud. "I'll shoot you."

"You aim to save me by shooting me?"

Serilda hissed in exasperation and angrily replied, "Don't try to confuse me. Yes, I'll shoot you. In the leg or in the foot but I'll make you get on your horse and go whether you want to or not." She wagged her six-shooter. "Hand me your rifle."

Fargo complied. It brought her nearer.

"Now move. And no tricks, you hear?"

"Whatever you say." Fargo held his hands out from his sides and started to turn. She took a half step, thinking he was going to do as she wanted, which brought her nearer yet. Quick as thought, he spun and grabbed her wrist with one hand and the Smith and Wesson with the other, his thumb under the hammer so if she squeezed the trigger, the revolver wouldn't go off.

"No!" Serilda cried, and tried to pull loose.

Fargo held firm. She went to swing the Henry at him and he gave her wrist a sharp twist, eliciting a bleat of pain. "Don't even try. I'll be nice so long as you are but try to hurt me and I'll knock you down." Even in the dark he could see that her eyes were flashing with barely contained fury.

"I believe you would. And here I liked you."

"I like you too," Fargo admitted. "But I'll leave when I'm damn good and ready. Savvy?"

Serilda glared.

"I want your word that if I let go, you'll put your six-gun away so we can talk. I'd like to know what's going on and I think you have some of the answers."

"I have all of them."

"Your word?"

"If you let go I promise I won't shoot you," Serilda said sullenly. "But you're making a mistake."

"I've made them before." Fargo released her arm and took the Henry. "Do we talk here?"

"In there," Serilda said, and motioned at the general store. "I don't want anyone to see us."

Nor did Fargo. She turned and he began to follow. Almost instantly she spun. Instinctively, he tried to duck but he wasn't fast enough. Pain exploded in his temple and his hat went flying. The blow sent him to his knees. His vision swam. He raised the rifle to ward off another blow but he wasn't attacked. Gritting his teeth, he shook his head to clear it. His surroundings came into focus: the back of the store, the weeds and grass, the dark, but no Serilda.

"Damn it." Fargo jammed his hat back on, heedless of the pain. She couldn't have gotten far. He glanced both ways but didn't spot her. Nor was she making for the woods. That left the general store. He stepped to the doorway. The inside was bottom-of-a-well black. He slowly roved from the rear to the front and back again. Either she was well hidden or she wasn't in there.

Fargo backed out. He was sick and tired of people disappearing on him.

About to head for the saloon, he froze when the night wind brought a new sound, a sound so haunting it prickled the skin at the nape of his neck.

It was the howl of a dog, a long, low ululating cry that seemed to come from everywhere and yet from nowhere.

Fargo turned every which way, trying to pinpoint where the howl came from, but couldn't. In his frustration he smacked the Henry.

It was time he got to the bottom of what was going on.

And he knew just where to start.

7

Over an hour had gone by. Fargo began to think he was wasting his time and she wouldn't show when the back door to the millinery opened and out snuck Gretchen Worth. She wore the same robe, tightly wrapped. Quietly shutting the door behind her, she looked at him and whispered, "I shouldn't do this but here I am."

"Nice perfume," Fargo said.

Gretchen moved away from the door. "Come with me." She walked toward the woods, her arms across her bosom, her head bowed in thought. Midway there she stopped and faced him. "Let's get one thing clear. I didn't come out here to tickle your fancy. I'm a lady and ladies don't do those sorts of things."

"Why did you come, then?"

"Because, confound it all, you're right. I *do* need a friend. I need one desperately. I'm in such dire straits I can hardly believe it."

"Lucky me."

"Don't. Please. The situation is too serious. Will you help me or won't you?"

Fargo stepped up close. "What's in it for me?"

"You can't mean . . ."

Grinning, Fargo ran a hand from her shoulder to her elbow. She didn't, he noticed, pull away. "Let me tell you what I've guessed and you tell me where I'm wrong. Harker and Landreth have abducted you and Esther and are holding you for money. They hired Moon and his gun crew to help and brought you here to lie low until it shows up."

"You're a good guesser. But you don't know the most important part, at least as far as I'm concerned." Gretchen gnawed her lower lip. "I wasn't abducted. I came along willingly. It's Esther they are pretending to hold until her parents pay them the five hundred thousand dollars they are demanding for her release."

The sum boggled. Now Fargo understood why James counted on spending the rest of his days living in luxury. But something else she said interested him more. "Why did you say they are pretending to hold her?"

Gretchen put a hand to her forehead and closed her eyes. "God, how could I let myself be talked into this?"

Fargo waited.

"Esther isn't being held against her will. This whole affair was her idea. The abduction, the demanding of the money. She intends to go off with James after they get it."

Fargo was confused. "She's helping him steal from her own folks?"

"They're in love, James and her. Her father is a banker, one of the richest men in San Francisco. He didn't approve of James. Called him a lazy gadabout and demanded Esther stop seeing him. So Esther cooked up her scheme."

Fargo was still confused. "How do they expect to get away with it? Her pa must know James won't hurt her."

"That's another part of her little plot. They've arranged things so someone else takes the blame."

"Who? Moon?"

Before Gretchen could answer, Fargo heard footsteps behind him and spun.

He didn't shoot, though. Not when he saw who it was.

Esther Mindel made no attempt to pull her robe about her. Not that it would have done any good, as sheer as it was. "Gretchen, what is the meaning of this? I woke up and saw you were gone so I came looking and here I find you talking

49

to—" She stopped. "Who are you, again? You're not one of Moon's men."

"The handle is Fargo."

"That tells me nothing. What do you do? Why are you here? And why are you meeting with my best friend in secret?"

"It's not what you think," Gretchen said.

"Frankly, I don't know what to think. You remember your promise to me, don't you? You're not going back on it?"

"No, never."

Fargo turned, draped his arm over Gretchen's shoulders and made as if he were kissing her on the ear when he was really whispering, "Play along." Then he said gruffly to Esther, "The lady and me want to be alone."

Esther didn't try to hide her surprise. "Did I hear correctly, Gretchen? You and this lout?"

Gretchen said nervously, "We talked earlier and he showed an interest. I find him handsome."

"But to meet him out here. Why, your mother would be scandalized. It just isn't like you."

"You're the only one who can attract a man?"

To Fargo's considerable amazement, Gretchen suddenly pressed herself against him and glued her mouth to his. Her lips were deliciously soft, her body delightfully warm. He tried to slide his tongue into her mouth and she bit down hard enough to almost make him cry out. When she broke the kiss she defiantly faced Esther with her hands on her hips.

Esther was as astonished as Fargo. "Now I've seen everything. All these years you've acted so pure." She laughed a vicious laugh. "I would never have guessed you had it in you."

"You must admit he's handsome."

"But he wears buckskins, for God's sake."

"Clothes aren't important."

"They are to me. What is he? A prospector? Or a backwoodsman? Haven't you heard they are animals?"

"I'm right here," Fargo said.

"You finally admit you're a woman and you pick *him*? Why not Roy Landreth? At least Roy has manners and breeding and knows how to dress."

"It takes a bitch to know a son of a bitch," Fargo said.

Esther looked at him in contempt. "I beg your pardon?"

"You wear fine clothes but I've known whores who are a lot better people than you'll ever be."

"How dare you," Esther sniffed. "Another insult and I'll have James and Roy deal with you, you ill-mannered bumpkin."

"Turn around and bend over."

"What on earth for?"

"So I can kick you in the ass."

Gretchen stepped between them. "Stop it. Esther, I like him. I'm asking you as your friend to go back in and leave us be. I won't be long. I promise."

"He insulted me."

"You insulted him."

"He has the manners of a goat."

"Please. I'm doing you a favor. Can't you do me this little one in return?" Gretchen put her hand on Esther's arm. "I never ask for much but I'm asking this of you now."

Esther's scowl was bone-deep. "Very well. But I don't approve of him. I don't approve at all." Her back ramrod straight, she wheeled and stalked to the millinery, slamming the door after her.

"Nice friend you've got there," Fargo said. "Does she always go around with a broom shoved up her . . ."

Gretchen put a finger to his mouth. "Enough. I played along with you to spare a scene. But I won't have you insult her. She's still my friend."

"What's your part in this?" Fargo asked.

"I came along to look after her."

"That's all?"

Gretchen sighed. "Esther and I have been friends since we

were little. We've always stuck by each other. I tried to talk her out of this but she refused to change her mind. Now the best I can do is stick with her and try to make it less of a mess than it already is."

Fargo admired this woman. He placed great value on friendship and so did she. He didn't have a lot of close friends and those he did he would do anything for. "You have sand," he complimented her.

"Thank you. Now if you'll excuse me, I better go in before she becomes madder than she already is."

"Wait." Fargo grasped her hand. "One last thing. How do Maxine and her family fit in?"

"Who?"

"The redhead and her dogs."

"I don't have any idea what you are talking about. Explain it to me later. I really must go." Gretchen went to turn but stopped and reached up and touched his cheek. "Thank you."

"For what?"

"For offering to help. I'm very much afraid that unless we're very careful, Esther's mad scheme will lead to violence."

"It already has. Or have you forgotten the stage driver?"

"I'll remember that poor man in my nightmares for the rest of my life." Gretchen hurried in.

Fargo went out to the street. Except for a light in the millinery and another in the saloon, Kill Creek was dark and desolate. The wind whipped out of the northwest, chilling him. He headed for the saloon.

The door to the butcher shop was open and as Fargo came abreast of it, from inside came a scuffing sound. Dropping his hand to his Colt, he peered in. He couldn't see much. The scuffing was repeated, from deeper in, he thought. Silently sideling in, he crouched.

Something swished over his head.

Fargo sidestepped and drew just as a large shape loomed

out of the darkness. It was the hooded figure he had seen at the stable and again in a window. There was another swish, and a hard jolt to Fargo's forearm sent the Colt skittering. Fargo bounded to one side and the figure came after him, swinging. Fargo raised the Henry in both hands and there was the clang of metal on metal. The blow was so powerful it jarred him. The man in the frock was enormously strong.

Fargo tried to aim the Henry but another blow knocked it from his grasp.

He crouched, hoping for a chance to palm the Arkansas toothpick. Something brushed his shoulder and thudded into the floor. Before the figure could swing again, Fargo sprang. He landed a punch to the hood that had no effect. He jabbed the man's gut but it was like hitting a wall. Then a backhand sent him tottering. He recovered and raised both fists.

The figure had vanished.

Suspecting a trick, Fargo backed toward the door where the light was better.

A minute crawled by. Other than voices from down the street, the ghost town was still. The butcher shop might as well be a morgue.

Another minute, and Fargo ventured to rove the floor, hunting for his weapons. He swung his boot from side to side and made contact with something.

The Henry. Scooping it up, he held it level while he continued to slide his boots back and forth. The Colt took longer to find. It was over near a corner. Rearmed, Fargo backed out of the shop. He didn't breathe easy until he was in the street.

Fargo pondered the attack. It made no sense. If the hooded figure was who he thought it was, why had the man tried to kill him? He would as soon be shed of this whole nonsense if not for Gretchen. And Maxine. And Serilda. Any one of them would do to spend the night with.

He walked on to the saloon.

James Harker and Roy Landreth were at the table. Moon and his men were over by the bar, and the moment Fargo walked in, Moon demanded, "Where the hell have you been, mister?"

Fargo told them about the figure in the butcher shop.

James came out of his chair. "It must have been whoever gave Esther that scare. Mr. Moon, I want someone keeping watch down at the millinery. The guard is not to go in but he is to make damn sure the ladies aren't harmed."

Moon nodded at Shorty and Shorty clomped out.

"We should have sent someone sooner," Landreth complained. "Instead we sit here squabbling with the hired help."

"I don't much like you," Moon said.

Landreth didn't respond.

"When you don't answer a man, that's an insult."

"Not that again," James said. "This constant squabbling is annoying. You would do well not to carp, given how much you stand to gain."

"If it wasn't for your jackass of a friend there, we'd get along just fine," Moon said.

Landreth started to rise but James put a hand on his shoulder. "Control that temper of yours." He turned to Fargo. "The issue now is what to do with you."

"You won't do a damn thing."

James held out a hand. "I'm afraid I'll have to ask you to turn over your revolver and your rifle."

"Like hell," Fargo said.

"Be reasonable. There are six of us. You wouldn't stand a prayer." James smiled. "Do as I ask and I promise that once this is over I'll return your guns and you can be on your way."

"No."

"You can trust me."

"You must think I'm loco."

"I think you are pigheaded."

Fargo kept his eyes on Moon and his men. The Henry was in his left hand, his right next to his holster.

James turned toward the bar. "Mr. Moon, would you do me the favor of having—"

From down the street came a crash and a whinny.

"What the hell?" Conklin exclaimed. "That came from the stable."

Fargo was past the batwing before the whinny died. He fairly flew, fear filling him, fear for the one thing in all the world that mattered. He reached the stable and dashed inside and an oath was torn from his lips.

The Ovaro had been taken.

Again.

8

If there was anything that made Fargo madder than having the stallion mistreated or stolen, he had yet to come across it. He saw no one in the direction of the bluffs so he ran around the corner toward the forest. No one was there, either.

Bewildered, and growing madder, Fargo returned to the front. By then James and Landreth and Moon and the others were there, and James Harker asked the obvious, "Someone took your horse?"

Fargo scanned the street.

"It wasn't one of us and it certainly wasn't the women," Landreth said. "Who else is in this godforsaken town?"

Fargo could think of three people: Maxine, Serilda and their pa. He scanned the empty street and slapped the Henry against his leg in frustration.

"Where could it have gotten to?" James voiced the very puzzlement Fargo was feeling. "A horse can't just disappear."

Fargo scoured the bluffs again. There was nothing at all to give a clue.

He bent and examined the ground but the jumble of recent prints thwarted him.

He went to go in the stable and Roy Landreth grabbed his arm.

"Hold on. There's still the matter of handing over your firearms. We'll take them now, if you don't mind, and even if you do."

Fargo snapped. In the blink of an eye he had the Colt out and up and slammed the barrel against Landreth's head. Landreth's bowler went flying and Landreth buckled at the knees and oozed to the ground like so much mud.

"Lord Almighty!" the hardcase called Tucker bleated. "Did you see that? I hardly saw his hand move."

"He's as quick as you," Beck said to Moon.

James was riveted in disbelief but now he went to slide his hand under his jacket.

Fargo pointed the Colt at him and thumbed back the hammer. "Try it and die."

James imitated a tree.

"I'm serving notice," Fargo said to all of them. "The next son of a bitch who gets in my way better have a hankering for the hereafter." He waited for one of them to say something and when no one did he twirled the Colt into his holster and looked at Moon. "How about you?"

"If I decide to I'll pick the time and the place. This ain't it."

Fargo took a stride but Moon wasn't done.

"One more thing. If and when I do decide, it won't be in the back. I am a lot of things but not a back-shooter."

Fargo remembered him shooting the unarmed driver, and wasn't impressed.

"Anytime you want."

The dust in the stable had been disturbed by all the comings and goings. There were so many tracks, reading sign was next to impossible. A jagged hole in the stall where the Ovaro had kicked it and furrows in the dirt told Fargo the stallion resisted. He suspected that whoever was to blame used a rope.

He hastened back out and around to the rear, ignoring the glares of Landreth, who was being helped to rise by James.

Fargo reckoned that the stallion *had* to be in the woods. There hadn't been time for the horse thief to take it anywhere else. He jogged to the tree line and stopped to listen. A beastly chorus filled the night air—the cries of coyotes, the shriek of a big cat.

Careful to place each boot quietly, Fargo entered the forest. There was no movement anywhere, no noises out of the ordinary. It was as if the earth had opened up and swallowed the Ovaro whole. He went another twenty yards and realized how futile it was. His best bet was to wait until daylight.

Simmering with rage, Fargo headed back. He came out of the trees and stopped. "You."

"I warned you and you didn't listen."

"Where's my horse, Maxine?" In the dark it would be hard for Fargo to tell her from her sister if not for the four-legged forms on either side of her. "I want it back and I want it back now."

"You don't listen very well."

Fargo took a step and two of the dogs snarled. He didn't care. "I won't tell you again."

Maxine's hair swirled in the wind, lending the illusion her tresses writhed like snakes. "You should have left when I told you to. Now they're here and there's nothing I can do. It's too late for your horse and it's too late for you."

"Stop talking in goddamn riddles. It's your pa, isn't he? He's the one running around in that hood. He jumped me in the butcher shop and now he's gone and taken my horse."

"Can you lift an anvil over your head with one hand?"

The question was so peculiar it threw Fargo off his mental stride. "What was that?"

"You heard me. Can you lift an anvil over your head with one hand?"

"What the hell does that have to do with my horse?"

"Just answer the question."

Fargo had been in more than a few blacksmith shops in his travels and he knew how heavy anvils were. A small one might weigh a hundred and twenty pounds, larger anvils upwards of three hundred. "I've never tried."

"He can."

"Who? Your pa?" Fargo took another step and three of the mastiffs growled and the fourth crouched low to the ground as if to spring. "Call your mutton-heads off."

"Have I introduced you?"

"To your dogs?"

"They have names." Maxine pointed at the mastiff farthest to her left and then at each in turn. "That's Thunder and then Lightning and this one over here is Storm and the last one is Cloud."

"Stupid names for dogs."

"I happen to like thunderstorms. I was going to name the last one Wind but I decided Cloud was better." Maxine put her hand on Lightning's head and the mastiff rubbed against her. "They do whatever I want them to."

"I haven't forgotten," Fargo said.

"Then why didn't you go? Serilda and me both tried to get you to and you stayed."

"I couldn't."

"Too bad." Maxine was quiet a bit, and then said almost sadly, "I don't want to do this. I argued with him but he has the last say. And he's right about not leaving any witnesses. We don't want the law to come nosing around. It has to be everyone and everything and we have to erase all the sign, after."

"There you go with riddles again."

"I'll make it plain, then." Maxine's tone hardened. "It's too late for you and it's too late for them. It's fitting you're first since you got here before they did. I'd be obliged if you'd give my dogs some sport."

"Sport?" Fargo said.

"Run. I'll give you to the count of thirty. Then it will be them or you and you know as well as I do that it'll be you."

Fargo was tempted to start shooting but he couldn't get all four before they reached him.

"One," Maxine said, and then in rapid cadence. "Two, three, four, five, six . . ."

Fargo wheeled and plunged into the woods. A log was suddenly in front of him and he barely vaulted over it. He avoided a boulder and skirted a thicket and heard Maxine give a strange trilling cry and knew it was the signal.

The mastiffs were after him.

A pine was to his left, an oak to his right. He chose the oak.

Jumping, he caught hold of a low limb and pulled himself high enough to hook his elbow over the branch. Then, holding tight to the Henry, he swung his legs up and over. Now he was straddling the limb with his back to the bole. Precariously balanced, he reached higher and got hold of another branch. As he was pulling himself up the undergrowth crackled and out spilled his canine pursuers. They had their noses to the ground and were sniffing. The first came to the oak, looked up, and howled.

Fargo jammed the Henry to his shoulder. The dogs were growling and pacing. One of them suddenly rushed at the oak and leaped at Fargo's roost but fell well short, its massive jaws snapping shut with a *crunch*.

Fargo laughed. He had outwitted the bastards; they couldn't get at him.

He fixed a bead on the dog that had jumped but it moved around to the other side of the tree. He took aim at another. But before he could thumb back the hammer, a whistle pierced the woods. The mastiffs promptly whirled and vanished into the benighted greenery.

Fargo waited. He wasn't about to let himself be tricked into climbing down with them still there.

From out of the brush came a melodious laugh. "You're a clever cuss, I'll give you that."

"Call them off, Maxine. You don't have to do this."

"Yes, I do. I may not amount to much but I can always say I've been a dutiful daughter."

"How many have you killed this way?"

Maxine didn't answer.

"Five? Ten? More?" Fargo heard a scraping noise on the other side of the oak. Holding on to a branch to keep from falling, he leaned as far out as he dared.

Once again, nothing.

Fargo settled back. There was nothing for it except to wait until they went away. The mastiffs were bound to give up eventually. They would get hungry or thirsty and drift off. Or would they, if Maxine stayed by their side? Then he remembered something else. Maxine had a six-gun. He needed to pinpoint where she was, so he called down, "You don't care much for those dogs, do you?"

She didn't reply.

"If you did you wouldn't set them on a man with a gun."

The stillness was unbroken.

A trick or not a trick? Fargo came to a decision. He lowered himself to the bottom limb, half expecting the dogs to come out snapping and growling, but none appeared. "I'll take as many of those curs with me as I can," he said to get Maxine mad enough to say something.

The continued silence persuaded Fargo she was gone and had taken the dogs with her. He lowered one leg. Nothing happened. He lowered the other leg. Still nothing. More convinced than ever, Fargo dropped to the ground.

The forest erupted. Snarling and slavering, the four mastiffs came at him from different directions.

Fargo streaked the Henry to his shoulder and fired. The slug caught a mastiff in the head and it tumbled right at him. He flung himself against the trunk to avoid it and felt the brush of a heavy body against his back; another dog had leaped and missed. He shifted as a third launched itself in the air and it smashed against him broadside, yelping when it hit. Quickly, Fargo darted around the tree to put it between them and him.

The fourth mastiff's teeth clamped onto his leg.

Fargo tried to wrench loose but the dog's fangs sank deeper. The pain was excruciating. He drove the Henry's stock at its eyes and the mastiff did as he hoped and scrambled back out of reach. He was bleeding but his leg was free and Fargo didn't waste a moment in barreling into the vegetation and flying for all he was worth. He shut out the pain and the blood and focused on running and nothing but running. The crack and pop of brush told him they had given chase.

A cluster of boulders loomed. Fargo veered to go around and then ducked behind the last. Hardly had he crouched than a darkling four-legged form bounded past. Then another. The third ran past on the other side. They were relying on sight and not their noses.

Fargo heaved upright and ran back the way he had come. It wouldn't take the dogs long to realize they had been tricked.

A howl rent the night.

Fargo glanced back but didn't see them. He faced front and there was the oak and the dog he had shot—and Maxine on her knees cradling its bloody head in her lap. She heard him and turned, unlimbering her revolver as she rose.

"You killed Thunder! Damn you to hell!"

Fargo hit her on the fly. He swung the Henry and clipped her across the head, and then he was past and bounding full out. He glanced back and saw one of the mastiffs hurtle out of the murk near the oak and abruptly stop. It had seen Maxine.

Grimly smiling, Fargo ran on. With any luck the other dogs would stop too.

He glanced up through the canopy at the North Star to get his bearings, and headed for Kill Creek. It wasn't long until he was in the open. Ahead were the benighted buildings. He thought maybe the racket would bring James Harker and Moon to investigate but he didn't see them. He reached the stable and sprinted around to the front. No one was there. He went over to the stage. Quickly, he clambered to the top and pressed flat. The seconds crawled and none of the dogs appeared.

Fargo breathed a little easier. Maxine must have called them off. He reached down and felt his leg and his hand grew wet with blood. He was bleeding badly. As much as he might want to, he couldn't stay there. He waited a while longer, just to be sure, and then lowered his legs over the side and dropped. His wounded leg nearly gave out but he stayed on his feet. Propping his rifle against the front wheel, he bent to examine the bite.

Light filled the doorway.

In came James and Landreth. Behind them were Moon, Conklin, Tucker and Beck, their six-shooters out and cocked.

"Here you are," James said. "It was a mistake to come back."

"Why?"

"We know it was you," Landreth declared. He pointed his cane at Moon and the others and then at Fargo. "If he so much as twitches, gentlemen, blow him to hell and back."

"What is this?" Fargo demanded.

"Your ploy with your horse didn't work," James said. "Now you will pay and pay dearly."

9

Fargo had no idea what he was talking about. He resented having the four revolvers pointed at him but for the moment there was nothing he could do.

"Where is she?" James demanded.

"Where the hell is who?"

"You know very well who," Landreth declared, advancing and raising his cane.

"Don't!" Moon hollered.

Landreth didn't listen, which was fine by Fargo because now Landreth was between him and the four hardcases. They couldn't shoot without Landreth taking a slug.

"You'll tell us, or so help me, I'll beat it out of you." Landreth swung the cane.

Fargo's hand streaked to his Colt even as he raised his other arm to ward off the blow. The pain made him grit his teeth. The next split second he rammed the Colt's barrel into Landreth's gut and Landreth started to double over. Spinning him around, Fargo hooked his left arm about Landreth's neck and jerked the dandy upright.

"No!" James cried. "Don't hurt him."

"Holster your hardware and be quick about it," Fargo said, gouging the Colt against Landreth's cheek.

James turned. "Do it! Under no circumstances is Roy to be harmed."

"He's your pard," Moon said. He nodded at the others and

twirled his pistols into his holsters. The others holstered theirs with less flourish.

"What about our pard?" Conklin said.

James faced Fargo and held his hands out from his sides. "There. See? You can let go of Roy."

Landreth tried to pull loose and Fargo gouged the barrel harder. "Stand still." Fargo focused on James. "Take a gander at my leg."

"Excuse me?"

"Look at my leg, you idiot."

All of them did, and James blurted, "You're bleeding!"

"I went looking for my horse and was attacked by a pack of dogs."

Fargo wasn't ready to mention Maxine and her sister and pa just yet. "They treed me and I just made it back."

Tucker said, "I told you I heard a dog barkin' but no one would believe me. I've got good ears."

"Then it couldn't have been him who busted Shorty's skull," Conklin said to Moon.

Fargo didn't hide his surprise. "Shorty's dead?"

It was Moon who answered. "Someone snuck up on him and caved his head in. Harker and Landreth reckoned as how it had to be you. I told them you didn't strike me as the back-killin' kind but they wouldn't listen."

"Shorty isn't the only calamity," James said. "Whoever killed him snuck into the millinery and carried Esther off. Gretchen was sleeping in the same room but didn't hear a thing."

"Where's Gretchen now?" Fargo had images of her in the hands of the figure in the hood.

"Here I am." She stepped into the stable, wearing her heavy robe. "James made me come with them. He says I dare not be alone."

"It's for your own good, my dear."

"At least let me go back and get dressed."

"In a minute." James smiled at Fargo. "You can release Roy. I believe your story."

"Do you, now?" Fargo angrily shoved Landreth so hard that he stumbled and would have fallen if James hadn't caught him and held him up. "The next time your gunnies point their hardware at me, you'll be the first one I shoot."

"It was an honest mistake."

"Go to hell." Fargo put his back to the wheel and eased down. He pried at his stained pant leg.

"What are you doing?" James asked.

Fargo thought he was talking to him and looked up. Gretchen was hurrying to his side. Kneeling, she moved his hands.

"Let me. My father is a doctor and I know a little about treating wounds."

She pulled the buckskin as high as it would go. "Oh my. It got you good."

The puncture marks were deep and still bleeding.

"Why were dogs after you, anyhow?" James asked. "There shouldn't be any here. No one has lived in Kill Creek in years. Isn't that what you told me, Mr. Moon?"

Moon nodded.

"This needs to be bandaged," Gretchen said to James. "He can come with me to the dress shop."

Landreth had recovered enough to straighten and scowl. "That's not necessary. One of us can do it."

"He's coming with me," Gretchen insisted, and rose. "Do you need help to walk, Mr. Fargo?"

Fargo was going to say no, that he wasn't helpless, but it would give him an excuse to be close to her. "I would be obliged, ma'am." Bracing against a spoke, he rose and grabbed the Henry, then slid his other arm over Gretchen's shoulders.

"Whenever you're ready."

"Send a man with them," James ordered Moon. "The rest of us will continue our search for Esther."

"There's no need for that," Gretchen said. "We can

66

manage, and you'll need every man you have to find her quickly."

Landreth wouldn't let it drop. "It's not proper you going with him alone."

"No. She's right," James said. "We need everyone. That includes you, Mr. Fargo, once you have that leg taken care of."

"Ask me nice and maybe I will."

Landreth reclaimed his cane. "The nerve you have. Don't think I'll forget that you've struck me, twice."

"Don't be such an ass," Gretchen said.

Landreth and James both appeared shocked. Moon, his hands on the butts of his Remingtons, laughed and said, "I reckon she told you."

Fargo limped out at Gretchen's side. Once they were out of sight, he kissed her on the cheek. "That's to repay you for the kiss you gave me earlier."

"Don't start with that again. I'm helping you out of the goodness of my heart, not because I want to make love to you."

"Your kiss said different."

"Honestly. Here you are, practically bled to death from a dog bite, and all you can think of is ravishing me?"

"I like that word. It wasn't the one I would use but I would take particular delight in ravishing you silly."

"You're hopeless. Do you know that?"

Fargo kissed her again, this time on the ear. "I'd say I have plenty to hope for, seeing as how you haven't smacked me."

"How can I when I'm carrying you?" Gretchen responded. "Although I notice you're not bearing down much of your weight. You didn't really need my help, did you?"

"No."

"Then why are we doing this?"

"So I can touch your body."

Gretchen laughed but immediately stopped and said, "Listen to me. Here you have me smiling and my best friend was just taken. I must be a wretched person."

"You look fine to me."

"That's not what I meant and you know it. Poor Esther. Where can she be?"

"You didn't hear or see a thing?"

"No, and that makes it even stranger. I couldn't sleep well. I was tossing and turning. The slightest sounds would wake me. Yet somehow, someone snuck into our room and carried Esther off without me hearing a thing. To say nothing of the fact that they murdered that poor cowboy."

Fargo knew Moon and his men weren't cowpokes. They wore slickers as cowboys did and wore boots and spurs and hats as cowboys did, but they no more made their living riding herd on cows than the queen of England. They were six-guns for hire, killers who squeezed the trigger for money.

"I'm so upset I don't know what to do," Gretchen had gone on. "I tried to warn Esther that no good would come of this insane scheme of hers but she wouldn't listen."

"Then it's on her, not you."

"True, I suppose. But that doesn't make it easier. I've been her friend for so long, we're like sisters." Gretchen sighed and her shoulders slumped. "I wish I could blot all this from my mind. I wish I could get a good night's sleep so I can think better come morning."

"I know a way." Fargo kissed her on the lips.

"Honestly. You're hopeless," Gretchen said, but not unkindly.

They neared the dress shop. Fargo had been keeping one eye peeled but saw no sign of Maxine and her dogs or Serilda or the figure in the hood. Once his leg was bandaged he intended to make it his first order of business to find them. Or maybe his second order of business.

Shorty's body lay where it had fallen. Fargo had Gretchen stop so he could examine it. The blow that killed the gun hand had been immensely powerful. It smashed Shorty's hat down onto his head with such force that the Stetson was driven into his brain pan and his brains had oozed from the cracks in his skull.

"How horrid." Gretchen looked away.

Fargo was about to rise when he noticed a bulge in the slicker. In all the excitement over Shorty's death and Esther being taken, James and Moon had forgotten about Shorty's six-shooter; it was still in his holster. Fargo held it up. It was a long-barreled Colt with six pills in the wheel. He held it out to Gretchen.

"What's this for?"

"Anyone tries to cart you off, you shoot the son of a bitch."

"I'm not much good with one."

"Stick it in their face and you won't miss."

"Can we go? I can't stand being near him."

"Lead the way." Fargo limped after her. They went down a short hall to a back room. A lit lantern was in the center. Spread out along opposite walls were their blankets. Trunks and bags were stacked in a corner.

"You see," Gretchen said, pointing at the blankets. "We weren't but ten feet apart yet I didn't hear a thing. How can that be?"

"Whoever took her clamped a hand over her mouth and got her out before she could struggle or scream."

"Sit down and I'll get to work. We have a waterskin from the stage, and I can tear up a towel for bandages."

Fargo sat where he could watch the door. There wasn't a window. He placed the Henry next to him and pried off his boot. It took some doing. His leg had swelled.

Gretchen sank onto her knees and set about exposing the dog bite and washing it. "How do you feel? As much blood as you've lost, I'm surprised you're not light-headed."

Fargo had had a bout or two since being bitten but at the moment he felt all right. He told her, adding, "I have something else on my mind."

"Not that again."

Putting his hands on her shoulders, Fargo drew her to him. He let the kiss linger but took no other liberties, and then sat back.

"You're awful free with your lips."

Fargo crooked a finger under her chin. She didn't resist. He kissed her again, longer and harder, then settled back with a grin. "Hurry up with that bandage. We have more kissing to do."

"Aren't you worried that whoever took Esther will come back?"

Fargo patted the Henry. "Let them."

"I don't quite know what to make of you. You're either a fool or braver than most."

The bandaging took a while. There was a lot of blood to clean up. It had dried and caked and took some scrubbing. Gretchen rummaged in a trunk and came back with a bottle of tincture of iodine. Saying it might sting a little, she applied the tincture to each of the puncture marks and wiped off the excess.

Fargo occasionally heard shouts from down the street. James and company were going from building to building, and from what he could tell, not having any success.

Gretchen produced a clean towel and scissors from a sewing kit. She was cutting the towel into strips when footsteps thumped in the hall and into the room came James Harker, Roy Landreth and Moon.

"Is everything all right, my dear?" James asked.

"Of course. Why wouldn't it be?"

"What on earth is taking so long?" Landreth brusquely demanded. "We've searched half the town already."

"I had to be sure the wound is clean so there's no risk of infection."

"Hurry it up so he can help us in the hunt."

"He should wait a while."

"Nonsense," Landreth said. "I won't leave him alone with you any longer than necessary."

Gretchen appealed to James. "You saw yourself how much blood he lost. He's weak and could collapse if he exerts himself too soon. Give him an hour to rest and he'll be fit enough to lend a hand."

"If you think it necessary he can have half an hour," James said. "But are you sure you'll be safe?"

"Safer than I would be without anyone here to protect me."

"Very well." James moved to the doorway. "Come on, Roy. She'll be fine. Not much can happen in that short a time."

"I don't like it. I don't like it at all." Landreth departed, scowling.

Moon was the last to leave. He grinned at Fargo and said, "They don't have a lick of sense, do they?" He sauntered out, his spurs tinkling.

"What did he mean by that?" Gretchen asked.

"Your friend Harker was wrong. A lot *can* happen in half an hour." Fargo smiled and reached for her.

10

Fargo half thought she might pull away but she didn't. He rimmed her soft lips with the tip of his tongue and her mouth parted. She was tentative at first, but as the kiss lingered on and his hands sculpted the contours of her body, her reserve broke and she melted into him. Her hands rose around his neck and her warm fingers pressed his skin.

"That was nice," Gretchen said dreamily. "You are a wonderful kisser. You must have had a lot of practice."

"A little," Fargo admitted.

Gretchen glanced anxiously at the doorway. "What if they should come back while we are . . ." She didn't finish.

"They won't. They're too busy looking for Esther." Fargo shifted and pulled her onto his lap.

"Some friend I am. I should be out there helping."

"You can join them after," Fargo said. He ran a hand through her hair, admiring the velvet feel of the strands.

"Are you sure half an hour is enough?"

Fargo chuckled. "Five minutes is enough so we can take our time."

"I don't know." Gretchen put her cheek on his shoulder. "I've never done anything like this before. I'm not reckless by nature."

"You're the one who said she would like to forget for a while," Fargo reminded her as he ran his right hand from her shoulder to her narrow waist. "There's no better way."

Gretchen looked him in the eyes. "What *is* it about you? I

mean, you're handsome and all. Maybe the handsomest man I've ever met. But that's no reason to throw myself at you."

"You call this throwing?"

"For me it is."

Fargo sensed that she was changing her mind. He covered her mouth with his and her breast with his hand. At his first squeeze she let out a fluttering moan. He pinched the nipple through her robe and felt it harden like a tack.

"Goodness, what you do to me."

"There's more where that came from." Fargo cupped her other breast and kneaded it.

"Oh God."

Deftly opening the robe, Fargo slid his hand underneath. He figured she would have a chemise or some other garment on but his fingers caressed bare skin. "You hussy, you," he teased.

"What? Oh. I didn't have time to unpack all I wanted. I don't usually sleep with nothing but a robe."

"Lucky me," Fargo said, and opened it wider. Her gorgeous mounds bulged free, round and full and inviting. He lowered his mouth to a nipple and flicked it with his tongue. Gretchen squirmed and pulled hard on his hair, nearly knocking his hat off. He switched to the other nipple and lightly nipped it while he squeezed and caressed both breasts. She breathed in low gasps and wriggled her bottom.

"I like that."

So did Fargo. He dallied at her melons a while and then remembered they had only half an hour. Taking hold of her hips, he said, "Part your legs." Her face flushed but she did as he wanted and he swiveled her around so she faced him. The robe came open all the way and he saw the flat of her belly and the golden thatch below. His manhood, already hard, became iron.

"What *is* it about you?" Gretchen wondered again.

"Let me know if you figure it out." Fargo shifted his hands from her hips to her bottom and dug his nails in.

Arching her back, Gretchen whispered, "You make me want to do things I shouldn't."

"Maybe it's my bandanna?"

Gretchen laughed and then gasped as he slid one of his hands from her buttocks to the junction of her thighs. He massaged down to her knee. Her skin was delightfully soft and deliciously warm. He cupped her, and his middle finger became moist. A flick of his fingertip set her to throwing back her head and moaning.

"You sure know how to please a girl."

"I'm just getting warmed up." Fargo kissed her and stroked her neck and rubbed her shoulder and slid his finger up inside of her.

"Ohhhh." Gretchen's eyelids fluttered.

Fargo added a second finger. She was wet for him, and when he pumped his fingers, she uttered tiny mews and ground against his hand. Her lips fused to his. He stroked and they kissed and her body grew hot to his touch. She panted as he licked her neck and bit her earlobe and traced the tip of his tongue from her throat to her cleavage.

Fargo undid his gun belt and set the Colt within easy reach. Prying at his pants, he let his manhood spring free.

Gretchen looked down and husked, "Oh my."

To Fargo's surprise and delight, she gripped his pole with one hand and cupped him down low with the other. He thought she might be prudish but she was hungry for it. When she slid her fingers higher and delicately ran her fingertip around and around, he almost exploded.

Now it was her turn to tease him. "Like that, do you?"

Fargo couldn't speak for the lump in his throat. He inhaled a nipple and worried it with his lips. With his thumb he rubbed her swollen knob. Her chest heaved from excitement and lust.

Easing his fingers out, Fargo put his hands under her and raised her high enough for his swollen member to slide between her legs. He ran the head of his organ along her wet slit and she shivered.

"God, I want you in me."

The feeling was mutual. With a sharp thrust, Fargo buried his pulsing sword to the hilt. Gretchen's head flew back and she opened her mouth wide. His hands on her pelvis, he commenced to pump his piston. He moved faster and she moved faster until the room became a blur. He started to close his eyes to better savor the explosion and caught movement, or thought he did, out in the hall. Forcing himself to focus, he placed his hand on his Colt.

"Why did you stop?" Gretchen asked, sounding upset. "Is something the matter?"

"No." Fargo hadn't realized he had. He resumed stroking but kept his hand on his revolver. She eagerly rose high on her knees and then impaled herself, again and again and again. Soon she was puffing and caked with sweat. Tilting her head back, she shut her eyes.

"I'm almost there."

Fargo would have been if not for his concern over who or what might be in the hall. He wondered if he had imagined it.

In a flood tide of passion, Gretchen's inner dam broke. She gushed and gushed, driving against him in relentless release. It was all Fargo could do to hold on to her. She cried out and it sent him hurtling over the brink of self-control.

Gradually, they subsided. Bit by bit they slowed until Gretchen collapsed against his chest. Fargo ran his hand over her damp hair and kissed her on the cheek.

"Any time you want to do that again, let me know."

Gretchen made a sound that resembled a goose being throttled.

"What?"

"When I said you were hopeless, I had no idea. Is that *all* you ever think of?"

"Only when I'm awake."

Gretchen laughed and kissed him on the chin. "Thank you. For a while you helped me forget and I'm grateful." She was about to say more but they both heard the slam of the front door. Scrambling up, she pulled her robe tight, crossed to the other side of the room, and leaned against the wall. Fargo hitched at his pants and got them up just in time.

In strode a tall drink of water in a slicker. "Moon sent me," Conklin said to Fargo. "He says you might want to come have a look-see at what we found. It has to do with your horse."

As much as Fargo would have liked to rest his leg a while more, he pushed to his feet, snatching the Colt and the Henry as he rose. "Lead the way." He started to follow and realized the mistake he was making. "Wait."

Conklin was already in the hall. "What?"

"We can't leave without her."

"She's a grown woman. She'll be fine. And Moon said to hurry. He won't like it if we dawdle."

"We can't let whoever took Esther take her. She'll only need a minute." Fargo smiled at Gretchen and she nodded and he closed the door behind him. In the dark he could barely see Conklin's silhouette. "Any sign of Esther yet?"

"Not a lick. Harker is fit to be tied." Conklin chuckled.

"You find that funny?"

"The way he's carryin' on, I do. Him and that Landreth, both. They gripe and cry about everything."

"I take it you don't like them much."

"Hell, mister. I've never cottoned to their kind. This is a job, nothing more. If they weren't payin' me, I'd have put windows in their noggins for all the aggravation they cause."

"Your boss feel the same?"

"Moon? He has even less use for them than me. Although now that—" Conklin stopped.

"Now that what?"

"Nothing. Where's that woman? How damn long does it take for her to throw on a dress?"

They stood in silence until Fargo, too, began to wonder what was keeping her. He knocked on the door. "You decent?"

"I'll be right out."

"Females," Conklin spat. "If there is anything more useless in this world, I have yet to meet it."

"I'm fond of them, myself."

"You can have them. I went six years in prison without one and didn't miss them a bit."

"You were behind bars?"

"A couple of times. Moon was once, too, for . . ." Once again Conklin stopped. "Listen, I'd be obliged if you don't tell him I told you. He tends to get mad when we run off at the mouth."

"He won't hear it from me."

The door opened. Gretchen had thrown on a plain brown dress and a brown bonnet. "Sorry to keep you gentlemen waiting."

"I ain't no gentleman, lady," Conklin said, and stalked off.

"What's bothering him?"

"He wishes that he looks as good in a dress as you do."

"I never know when you're serious."

Quiet gripped Kill Creek. The wolves had stopped howling, and the coyotes had ceased yipping. Save for the hoot of a solitary owl, the mountains might be lifeless. Conklin led them past the saloon to the stable. Someone was already there; light spilled out of the double doors. "Take a gander," he said to Fargo.

Moon was there with Tucker and Beck. So was James and Landreth. When Fargo entered they looked at him and then at the stall the Ovaro had been in.

The Ovaro was back.

"What the hell?" Fargo blurted. He hurried over and brought the stallion out. He checked for wounds. He examined all four legs. Then he patted it on the neck and said, "This makes no kind of sense."

"It doesn't to me, either," James said. "We were hunting for Esther and I happened to look in here and there your animal was. I know you couldn't have done it because you were with Gretchen."

Moon was scratching his stubble. "What kind of horse thief steals a horse and then brings it back?"

77

"I know the answer," Landreth said.

Everyone looked at him and James said, "You do?"

Landreth pointed his cane at Fargo. "He's in league with whoever has Esther."

"How in hell do you figure that?" Moon said.

"Simple. Stealing his horse was a ruse. They only pretended to in order to distract us and keep us at the stable while they killed Shorty and abducted Esther."

"That's preposterous," Gretchen said.

"Is it?" Landreth rejoined. "Think about it. Why else did they bring his horse back? A fine animal like that?"

Tucker said, "I wouldn't give him back if I stole him."

"Me either," Beck chimed in. "He's about the prettiest horse I ever did see."

Landreth turned to James. "You can see I'm right, can't you? We should demand he tell us where Esther is and if he won't, give him to Moon and have Moon persuade him to talk."

"I don't know," James said. "I don't think he was shamming when he found his horse was gone."

"I tell you he deceived us. We should confine him until we're done here and decide what to do with him when we leave."

Fargo turned and leveled the Henry. "I'd like to see someone try." He would be damned if he would let them lock him away somewhere.

"You're being absurd," Gretchen said to Landreth. "He's our friend and you treat him like this."

"He's your friend, maybe. He certainly isn't mine. Anyway, you don't have a say," Landreth informed her.

The bickering might have gone on longer if not for an unexpected interruption: a round object came sailing in the open doors. It bounced and rolled and skittered to a stop, and Gretchen shrieked.

She had good cause.

11

Fargo was as stunned as everyone else. The head had been ripped from Shorty's body, not severed. Jagged strips of skin and flesh edged the neck, and Shorty's lifeless eyes were fixed on the rafters in glazed emptiness.

"Dear God!" James exclaimed in horror.

Landreth looked fit to be sick.

Moon was the first of the gun crowd to come out of his shock. He ran up to the head, swore luridly, then bellowed, "Come on, you jackasses." Drawing his Remingtons, he raced from the stable.

Conklin, Tucker and Beck overcame their shock, drew their own artillery, and ran out after him.

Gretchen had turned away and pressed her hands to her face. "How could anyone do that?"

James went to her and put his arm around her shoulder. "Try to be strong. We'll take you back and Roy will stay with you while I get to the bottom of this and Esther's disappearance." He glanced at Fargo. "What about you?"

"I'll be along in a minute."

The two city men ushered Gretchen out. She glanced back worriedly at Fargo and he smiled to reassure her.

No one had thought to do anything about the head. Fargo walked over to it.

The proper thing to do, he supposed, was to pick it up and carry it back to the body so the parts could be buried together. He kicked it into a corner.

Fargo turned to the Ovaro. Right before the head was thrown into the stable, he'd noticed that something had been draped over his saddle: his saddlebags. Mystified, he put his hand on them. "How the hell did you get here?" The last he saw, they had been on the table in the saloon. A flap had been undone. He looked inside. His puzzlement growing, he pulled out a crumpled piece of paper. Someone had written on it in a feminine hand. The message read:

This is your last chance. They'll be mad at me but I've brought your horse and your effects back. Go, please, before it's too late. I doubt I'll be able to help you again. I know him. The killing will start soon.

Serilda

Fargo put the paper in his saddlebags and stared at the Ovaro. If he had any sense, he would do what she wanted. He would throw his saddle on the stallion and put a lot of miles between them and Kill Creek. So far all he had suffered was a dog bite and some bruises but he might go through a lot worse if he stayed.

Fargo slid his saddle blanket off the stall and swung it up and over the stallion. He smoothed it down and then swung the saddle on. After doing the cinch he tied on his saddlebags and was ready. Stepping into the stirrups, he rode from the stable and reined down the middle of the street—not away from Kill Creek, but into it.

Moon and his pack were barreling from building to building. They came out of one as Fargo was passing, and stopped.

"You leaving?" Moon asked.

"No."

"Then why saddle your cayuse?"

"From now on where I go, it goes," Fargo informed him. He would be damned if he would let it be taken again.

"No sign yet of the bastard who tore Shorty apart but we'll find him," Moon said. "He thinks this is his town and he can hide but he'll find out different." Moon motioned and he and his brother wolves ran on.

Fargo drew rein at the millinery.

Just then James emerged. "Ah. You've joined us. Excellent. How about if we search together while Mr. Moon and his friends conduct their hunt? Two search parties are better than one."

"Gretchen?"

"Distraught, but she'll recover. Roy will watch over her and see that she doesn't share Esther's fate." James blanched. "My sweet Esther. She's everything to me, Mr. Fargo. I love her heart and soul." He headed toward an abandoned house.

Fargo swung down and led the Ovaro by the reins. As they walked he shucked the Henry from the saddle scabbard.

"Yes, sir," James rambled on. "A woman like Esther comes along but once in a man's lifetime. You wouldn't believe the sacrifice she has made in the name of our love."

"Try me."

"She's given up everything on my behalf. Her parents, the life she was living—she threw them all aside in my favor. If that's not love, I don't know what is."

Fargo forgot himself and said, "Love or greed?"

James glanced over sharply. "Greed? What has Gretchen been telling you?"

"She didn't say a thing," Fargo lied. "I overheard mention of a lot of money."

"What we've done we did out of love," James said, and put his hand to his chest. "Our love is sublime, Esther's and mine. It is Romeo and Juliet and Anthony and Cleopatra all over again."

"Who?"

"Surely you've read William Shakespeare? Even if you haven't, you must know what true love is."

"Love is what a man calls it when he wants it regular. She must be a wildcat in bed."

James stopped and scowled. "I beg your pardon? I'll thank

you not to be so vulgar. Esther is a lady. I love her for her heart and for her mind and her wonderful personality."

"What about her body?"

"Love is more than *that*. Are you going to stand there and tell me you've never felt it, not once in your entire life?"

"I've felt a twinge or two," Fargo admitted.

"Well then. You know exactly how I feel about Esther, and why I would do anything for that woman. Now please. We must find her, and quickly. I shudder to think what might happen to her in the hands of whoever murdered poor Shorty."

The next house proved to be empty. So did the cabin after that. Moon shouted to them from the other end of the street, asking if they had found anything, and James yelled back that they hadn't.

Fargo was on the watch for Maxine and her remaining three dogs but apparently she showed herself to him only when no one else was around. The same with the hulking figure in the frock and hood.

"Where can she be?" James anxiously asked for the fiftieth time as they came to the last house. "It's as if she vanished into thin air."

"There's a lot of that going on."

"You say the strangest things." James clomped onto a rickety porch and opened the door. It creaked on hinges long neglected and wouldn't open all the way. "Esther?" he called out. "Are you in here?" Something scuttled past him and he jumped and bleated, "Look out! It's a rat!"

The animal ran past Fargo's boots and into brush along the porch. "I don't usually run from rabbits or rodents."

James was staring at the brush as if afraid the rat would come back out. "You're mocking me, aren't you? Did you see the size of that thing? It was longer than my foot."

"A lot of rats grow that big. It's nothing to pee your pants over."

"You're not nearly as funny as you think you are. For

your information, I know of people who were bitten by rats and became deathly ill. What do you think of that?"

"I think where there's one rat, there's liable to be a lot more."

James peered into the house and hesitated. "That's right. They live in colonies, don't they? There could be hundreds of the vile things. Perhaps thousands." He drew a pocket pistol. "Be ready, just in case."

"Have you ever tried to shoot a running rat?"

"I can't say as I have. Why?"

"They're as hard to hit as a jackrabbit. Your best bet is to stomp them to death."

"And get their guts all over my shoes? No, thank you. Mine are made from the finest Italian leather." James inched forward and peeked around the door. "It's so dark in here."

Fargo almost said "Boo" to see what he would do. "We don't have all night."

"All right." James went in but took only a couple of steps. "I don't hear anything. Do you?"

"Oh, hell." Fargo shouldered past. As near as he could make out, he was in a parlor or sitting room. A narrow hall led to a small kitchen. A squat shape in the corner caused him to level the Henry but it turned out to be a stove. The whole house had a dank, earthy scent, the result of neglect, he reckoned and went back out.

James was anxiously waiting. "She's not in there? Damnation. I dare say our search will prove as fruitless as the last time. Where in the world can they have taken her? Into the forest?"

Fargo was about to suggest they look over at the bluffs when a faint sound fell on their ears. So faint, he barely heard it—a low wavering howl.

"Was that a wolf?" James asked.

"A dog."

"Where did it come from? I couldn't tell."

Fargo looked down at his boots. He would swear the howl had come from under the ground. He thought of how Serilda and her family kept disappearing, and of the cool air he'd felt on his face in the back room of the saloon, and then of the dank smell in the house, and he slapped his forehead and swore.

"What's wrong? Did you see another rat?"

"I'm an idiot. I should have figured it out sooner."

"Figured out what?"

"I thought there must be a hidden door in or out of the saloon but I was wrong. They're not going through the walls."

"What on earth are you talking about? I'm utterly confused."

"Go fetch a lantern." Fargo stepped out on the porch, careful to avoid a hole where the wood had rotted.

"I'm the one in charge. Give me one good reason why I should go and not you?"

Fargo trained the Henry on him. "This holds fifteen reasons."

James smiled and extended his pistol. "I have a gun too. You'll need to do better than that."

"Esther."

"What about her?"

"Do you want to find her or not?"

"That's a stupid question. I just got through telling you a short while ago how much she means to me."

"Then why the hell are you arguing? Fetch a lantern and I'll show you where they took her."

"They who?"

"The lantern, damn it."

"All right, all right. I'll be right back." James hurried off, saying over his shoulder, "But if this is a trick you'll regret it. I'm not someone you want to trifle with."

Fargo wondered why it was that so many dandies were so full of themselves. Harker and Landreth acted tough but they wouldn't last two seconds against an Apache or Comanche out to slit their throats. They were baby chicks pretending to be roosters. Put them in the wild without food and water and they would die within a week.

Up the street, Moon had just come out of the general store, Tucker and Beck in his wake. They saw James and moved to meet him.

Fargo decided not to wait. Going back in, he went down the hall to the kitchen. It was there that the dank smell was strongest. He began to thump the floor with his boot. He was near the stove when a thump rang hollow. A few more thumps and he dropped to his hands and knees and pried at the boards with his fingers. It took some doing. The trapdoor fit snugly but he lifted it out and set it down. From below came the musty odor of dirt. He lowered his legs and felt the rungs of a ladder. Carefully applying his full weight, he descended below the floor, reached up, and pulled the trapdoor shut after him.

He'd changed his mind. He would do better alone. James would be next to worthless and would only give them away.

Light bathed the cracks above him.

"He's not here," James said.

"Now the scout has up and vanished." That was Moon.

"I don't understand it. I think he had figured something out. He talked as if he knew where Esther is."

"Maybe he wanted to be shed of you." This time it was Conklin. "He tricked you into going for a lantern and you fell for it."

"What now, gentlemen?" James said. "I am open to suggestions."

"You should go check on your pard and that blond gal," Moon suggested. "We'll be along in a minute."

Shoes scraped but stopped short of the hallway. "Before I go, Mr. Moon, I must say how disappointed I am in your choice of a place to hide until the ransom arrives. Kill Creek, indeed. We've had nothing but trouble from the moment we got here." The shoes scraped away.

"You should let me shoot him," Conklin said.

"Not until his man shows up with the money."

Tucker asked, "What do you make of what's been goin' on? Why Shorty, for God's sake?"

"You know who did it as well as I do. She said she could keep him under control but she can't."

"We never should have trusted her," Beck said, then blurted, "Hold on! Don't get mad. I didn't mean anything. I know how powerful fond you are of her."

"Shut the hell up and let's go."

The light dimmed and Fargo was left in black darkness. He pushed on the trapdoor but it wouldn't budge. He pushed again, harder. It felt as if it was caught somehow. He braced his shoulder and was set to exert all his strength when a rustling sound set his skin to crawling.

Something, or someone, was below him.

12

Skye Fargo listened with held breath to the rustling, which grew louder and then stopped directly under him. He swore he could hear heavy breathing. He imagined that whoever or whatever it was knew he was there and he firmed his grip on the Henry. After what seemed an eternity of suspense, the rustling resumed, and it and the heavy breathing faded away.

Fargo waited a minute to be sure, then lowered one boot and then the other, testing each rung. At last his feet came down on solid ground. He groped and found an earthen wall. He had a choice of two directions and went in the direction the rustling had gone.

Kill Creek sat on top of a mine. Fargo could recollect two or three similar instances, including one in the Rockies west of Denver where several buildings buckled when the mine shaft under them collapsed.

How extensive these tunnels were, he couldn't say. He reckoned they ran the length of the town, if not longer, and there must be branches here and there where veins of ore had been followed until they petered out.

He was annoyed at himself for not figuring it out sooner. It should have dawned on him that given that Kill Creek was built during the gold rush, there might be a mine. He'd taken it for granted that the diggings at the bluffs were the reason for the town's existence.

Fargo went slowly. He didn't care to stumble on whoever or whatever had passed by earlier. His eyes adjusted enough that the walls were outlines against the black. He kept his left hand on the left wall as he went, and suddenly his fingers came on empty space. He was at a fork. If his sense of direction wasn't completely askew, the new branch led toward the diggings. He took it and soon the tunnel narrowed and the ceiling lowered to where his hat scraped. He was about to turn back when an acrid scent tingled his nose. A few yards more and he detected a pale patch up ahead.

Light.

Fargo slowed. He had to crouch to avoid having his hat knocked off. Another forty feet and the passage curved. He peered past the bend and saw a lantern hanging on a peg. He also heard voices.

Fargo crept forward. He reminded himself that it wasn't just the man in the hood he had to watch out for. There was Maxine, mad over the death of her dog, and the other three mastiffs. If they cornered him down there, he would be hard-pressed to survive.

There were two voices, and both were female. He recognized one and then the other. They came from the left, from another branch, he thought, but it was a chamber. Crouching, he took off his hat and put his eye to the opening. He wanted to hear what they said.

The chamber was roughly oval and about ten feet across. A lantern over on the far wall glowed bright. Huddled on her knees, bound ankles and wrist, was Esther Mindel. Her sheer robe was torn, exposing a creamy thigh, and she was streaked with dirt and grime, as if she had been dragged. She was glaring at the woman pacing back and forth in front of her and saying, "What do you hope to get out of this? It's horrid, what you've done."

Serilda stopped pacing and faced her. "I didn't do it. He did."

"Who is he, anyway? I've never seen anyone so hideous."

"He's my pa."

"Good Lord. How did it happen? What could have caused him to be the way he is?"

"I'm not here to talk about him. I came to decide whether I'll help you or not."

"Why wouldn't you?" Esther anxiously asked. "If you have a shred of human decency—"

Serilda held up a hand. "Stop right there. Don't pretend you're any better than me when you're not. I know the truth about you."

"Oh?"

"About your plan to steal money from your folks. Half a million dollars for you and your lover to live in luxury the rest of your lives." Serilda shook her head. "At least my pa has an excuse. What's yours?"

"Where did you hear so fabulous a tale? It's absurd."

"Don't insult me," Serilda said. "I know it's true and so do you. It's the reason you and your friends are here. But you didn't count on this, did you? You didn't count on being betrayed."

Esther rose straighter. "Betrayed? By whom?"

"It's not important now. What matters is: do I help you live or leave you here to die?"

"Your father intends to kill me?"

"I'm surprised he hasn't already. He's killed one of the others. Ripped the man's head clean off."

"Oh, God. It wasn't James, was it? James Harker? Do you know who he is? Please tell me he's still alive."

"Relax. Your lover is fine. My pa killed one of the men James hired to help him."

"Why?"

Serilda didn't answer. She resumed her pacing again and said, "What to do? What to do? Do I let him bash your brains out or wring your neck or do I save you from your own folly?"

"I've done nothing to deserve this. I've never hurt you or

89

your family. What does your father have against me, anyway?"

"You haven't paid attention. Maxine struck the deal. But she should have known. She can't control him. No one can. Not when it comes to this mine."

"You're not making any sense. Who's Maxine?"

Fargo glanced back down the passage to be sure no one or nothing was sneaking up on him.

"Most folks would say that neither of them are in their right mind," Serilda had continued. "He kills most everyone who comes here, which is why I try to warn them off. Those he doesn't kill, she usually sets her pack on."

"She who? Maxine?"

"You haven't met her yet. She's off burying one of her precious dogs. You're lucky. She has a different reason for wanting you dead, and she will kill you quicker."

"Please. What are you talking about?" Esther shifted. "Cut me free. I'll get the others and be gone as quickly as they can hitch the team to the stagecoach."

Serilda looked at her. "What about the money? You'll just up and leave and give it up after all the trouble you've gone to?"

"My life is more important."

"I wish I could believe that. But I suspect what you'll really do is try to convince your lover and the others to come down here and kill off me and my family. I can't have that. They've done a lot of bad things but they're still my pa and my sister."

"I give you my word. I'll leave Kill Creek and take everyone else with me. As God is my witness."

"Ah," Serilda said.

"Wait. What does that mean?"

Serilda said rather sadly, "It means I don't have a choice. You think that you're in control but you're not. Your darling James and his friend . . ." She paused. "What's his name again? The one who carries a cane?"

"Roy Landreth."

"They're in over their heads. It would have been better for all of you if you hadn't come up with your brainstorm." Serilda turned to leave but stopped at a question from Esther.

"Have you ever been in love?"

Fargo saw a hurt expression come over Serilda. She didn't turn to face Esther as she said, "Once. Years ago. I was very young and there was this boy I was fond of. I reckon it's not love in the way you mean but I cared for him with all my heart, just the same."

"Where is he now?"

Serilda closed her eyes and bowed her head. "Dead."

"You know what love is, then. How when you care for someone you'll do anything for them. My father and mother disapprove of James. They don't want me to have anything to do with him. But I love him. I can't leave him any more than I can stop breathing. So, yes, I came up with the idea of being held for ransom so that he and I can go off and live the rest of our lives together. Is that so bad?"

Serilda gazed over her shoulder. "Ever been where there is snow?"

"Plenty of times. Why?"

"When you stand at the top of a hill and pack snow into a ball and set it rolling, it doesn't always roll in a straight line."

"What's your point?"

"That you set a snowball to rolling and now it is going where it wants and there is nothing you can do to stop it."

Esther swore. "You keep confusing the hell out of me. You say your father and sister aren't in their right mind, but if you ask me, neither are you."

"You make it easy," Serilda said.

Putting his hat back on, Fargo waited until she was almost to the opening before he stepped into it with the Henry pointed at her belly. "Afraid not."

Serilda's hand flicked at the Smith and Wesson stuck in the top of her britches.

"Don't be stupid."

"You'd shoot me after all I've done to help you?"

"I'll shoot anyone who tries to shoot me." Fargo reached out and relieved her of the six-gun. He motioned for her to back away and she complied, raising her hands.

"How did you get down here?"

"I fell down a badger hole." Fargo kept motioning and she kept backing up until they came to the other side. "Untie her."

Esther was beaming. "Thank God. I was beginning to think no one would find me. Is James with you?"

"He's off fighting rabbits." Fargo thumbed back the Smith and Wesson's hammer. "I won't tell you twice, Serilda."

With surprising calm, she responded, "You squeeze that trigger and my pa and my sister will hear and come on the run. You don't want that."

"Hell, I don't want any part of any of this mess," Fargo said. "But your sister took my horse and your pa tried to kill me so I'm in it whether I want to be or not."

"You won't shoot me. Not an unarmed female, you won't."

"What makes you so sure?"

"I'm a good judge of character. I can see it in your eyes. You're not a cold-blooded killer."

"Maybe I'm not. But I'll sure as hell rap you over the noggin if you don't do as I say." Fargo was keenly aware that her father or Maxine and the mastiffs could show up at any moment.

Serilda squatted and pried at the knots. "My pa tied these awful tight. I could do it faster if I had a knife."

"I have one." Fargo bent to palm the toothpick. Too late, he glimpsed Serilda's hand sweep up and out. He tried to dodge but was struck full in the face by the handful of dirt she had scooped up. Dirt got into his eyes, into his nose, into his mouth. He coughed and blinked and backpedaled in case she came at him.

"She's getting away!" Esther cried.

Fargo's vision cleared in time for him to see Serilda dart

into the tunnel, taking the lantern with her. He gave chase, wiping at his eyes with his sleeve. She looked back and laughed and dashed the lantern to the ground. There was a shower of sparks and puffs of smoke and the tunnel was plunged in darkness.

Her feet pattered off.

"Damn." Fargo tucked the Smith and Wesson under his belt and hurried back. He crossed to where Esther was on her side, furiously struggling to break free.

"Did you stop her?"

"She got away."

"You're next to worthless," Esther criticized without slackening her effort. "Now she'll tell that lunatic pa of hers and we'll be lucky to make it to the surface alive."

Fargo drew the Arkansas toothpick. He was about to cut the rope around her ankle when seemingly from the bowels of the earth wafted a piercing howl.

"Did you hear that?"

"My ears work fine." Fargo slashed the rope and raised the knife to free her wrists.

"Hurry. You must take me to James. I'll tell him about these shafts and he can come down and wipe these lunatics out."

Fargo held the toothpick poised to slice. "The best thing to do is to leave Kill Creek."

"I can't do that and I suspect you know it. Now hurry, damn it, before it's too late."

It already was.

From the tunnel came a growl.

13

Fargo whirled. He thought it was a dog. But then he saw the figure hunched over in the opening. Its size, the fact it was on two legs, the suggestion of a frock and a hood—he jammed the Henry to his shoulder.

Esther screamed.

The figure sprang from sight. Fargo started to go after it but Esther screeched his name in stark fear.

"Wait! Don't leave me!"

Reluctantly, Fargo returned to her side. He cut the last rope and helped her to stand.

"That monster tied me so tight, he cut off the blood." Esther rubbed her wrists and said gratefully, "Thank goodness you came along when you did. You have to get me out of here."

"Was that who brought you down here?"

"Yes. I was sleeping and felt something over my mouth. I woke up to find him carrying me as easily as I might carry a flower. He's hugely strong, that monster."

"Why do you keep calling him that?"

"You haven't seen his face yet or you wouldn't ask. I swear. He's so grotesque, he turns your stomach." She started to go past him but he held out an arm.

"I should go first. I have the guns."

"I want a weapon too. Don't worry. My father made me go quail and rabbit hunting with him when I was a girl. I hated it but I learned to shoot."

Fargo was about to say no but at close range the Colt was lethal as the Henry. He held out the rifle.

"Thanks." Esther took it and pressed the stock to her shoulder. "It's heavier than I expected." She gripped the lever as if to work it.

"There's already one in the chamber." Fargo moved to the opening and peered out. As near as he could tell, the tunnel was empty.

"Which way?" Esther asked. "I was so scared when he carried me down here that I didn't pay much attention."

Fargo debated. If they went right it would take them the way he had come. He should be able to find his way back to the ladder he had used but the trapdoor was stuck. There were bound to be others, so he went left.

Esther walked so close, she brushed his back with every step. "Do you hear anything?" she nervously whispered.

"I might if you hush up."

"Sorry. I'm scared."

Fargo didn't blame her. He was on edge too. He went slowly, the dark pressing in on them. Presently they came to a bend and had another choice to make.

"These damn tunnels go on forever," Esther remarked. "We could wander around here for a year and not find our way out."

"I doubt that." Fargo faced to the right and then the left. From the left came a suggestion of breeze. Left it was. He took a step and was bumped hard in the back.

"Sorry."

"You need to calm down."

"Fat chance. I've always prided myself on my self-control but I've never been through anything like this. Ironic, isn't it? There wasn't supposed to be anyone here. Moon assured us there wasn't."

"He did, did he?"

"Yes. It was his idea to come to Kill Creek. He said we would be safe, that no one would think to look for us here.

He and his men even covered the stage tracks with brush and whatnot to be sure no one could track us."

Fargo doubted that would stop a seasoned tracker. It sure wouldn't throw him off. "How did Moon and you hook up?"

"Not me, silly. James had Roy ask around in some of San Francisco's more disreputable dives. Roy was very discreet. He merely said he wanted to hire someone who didn't care about which side of the law they worked on. The one name that cropped up again and again was Moon's."

"And then you went and dragged Gretchen into it."

Esther's tone became flinty. "How much do you know, exactly? It sounds to me as if someone has been talking out of school."

Fargo had blundered. He covered his mistake by saying, "I heard you and Serilda talking back there."

"Is that her name? She never said. I guess you've put two and two together and think you have everything worked out. But you're wrong. I didn't drag Gretchen into this. She offered to come to help protect me."

"You could have told her not to."

"Why would I do that? She's my dearest friend in all the world."

The section of tunnel they were in was inches thick with dust. The wall, when Fargo touched it, crumpled to the lightest touch. He realized he hadn't seen any support beams in a while. "We better go easy. A loud noise could bring the roof down."

"I saw a rat earlier. And there was a spiderweb big enough for a spider the size of a dinner plate."

The tunnel floor was littered with clogs of dirt and rocks, the tunnel roof pockmarked with the holes they fell from.

"God, I hope we get out soon," Esther whispered.

Fargo spotted something flush with the right wall. He reached out and felt rungs. "A ladder," he informed her. He put his foot on the bottom rung and it broke with a loud crunch.

"No!" Esther bleated. "Not when we're so close."

Fargo tested the next rung. It held, and he gingerly applied his boot to the third. It creaked but it held, too. The same with the rest. He climbed until his hat bumped an obstruction. It was another trapdoor. He pushed but it wouldn't budge. He put his shoulder to it and pushed harder. It barely moved.

"Hurry up, will you?"

"It's stuck."

"Hit it with your pistol."

"The hell I will."

"I'll hand up your rifle and you can hit it with that."

"The hell you will."

"Are you worried about damaging them? Staying alive is more important than your silly guns."

"My guns keep me alive," Fargo set her straight.

Fargo braced himself and tried again. He was worried the rungs would break but they didn't. This time the trapdoor moved a fraction, causing dust to rain down.

"James would have had it open by now."

"James can't open his fly without help."

"Why do you keep belittling him? He's as fine a man as ever drew breath. And he knows to chew with his mouth closed."

"You care about how he eats?"

"It's a sign of breeding. Certainly I care. A woman can't marry just any bumpkin off the street."

"To some gals chewing isn't important."

"It is if she wants a happy marriage. A woman must look for qualities that please her." Esther paused. "Take me, for instance. I wanted a gentleman. I wanted someone who waited on me hand and foot and would do whatever I asked of him."

"You'd make a great bullwhacker."

"Aren't they those men who handle teams of oxen? Are you saying my James is an ox?"

"I'm saying if you two marry, you'll wear the britches."

97

Esther sniffed. "I should be offended but I'm not. Do you know why? Because I *will* wear the pants. I've always gotten my way in this world and I don't intend to stop just because some man has taken it into his head he can't live without me."

"So much for true love."

"Oh, please. Just because a woman is in love doesn't mean she must stop using common sense. Marrying the wrong man can make a woman miserable for life."

"So can marrying the wrong woman."

"Are you going to talk or get us out of here?"

Fargo put both hands flat against the door and tried a third time. The door rose a couple of inches. Through the gap poured a torrent of dirt, getting into his face and down his neck.

"Did you hear that?" Esther breathlessly asked.

Fargo listened. All he heard was the dry hiss of dirt and the patter of a few stones. "Don't distract me."

"There's something in this tunnel with us, I tell you. An animal, I think."

"If it bites you, tell me." Fargo applied his shoulder to the trapdoor yet again, exerting every sinew in his body. He was rewarded with the rasp of hinges and a new cascade of dirt. A rock the size of an apple struck him on the arm. Five, six, seven inches the trapdoor rose—and wouldn't go any higher.

Esther was coughing and swatting at the dust. "*Must* you get it all over me?"

Fargo climbed one more rung and put his entire back to the trapdoor. His hands against the tunnel wall, he heaved. More dirt and stones fell over and around him. Suddenly there was a *crack* and the trapdoor gave way, flying up so fast he nearly lost his balance. Cool night air washed over him and he gazed up at a star-filled sky.

"You did it!" Esther squealed.

Fargo started to climb out.

"Where are you going? You're going to leave me down here by myself with that madman on the loose?"

Fargo sighed and went down. As he stepped off the ladder she shoved the Henry at him. Hopping onto the second rung, she scampered up with surprising agility. Near the top she stopped.

"Did you hear that?"

"I didn't hear a damn thing."

"Over that way," Esther said, pointing down the tunnel.

Fargo turned. There was nothing, nothing at all. He turned back to tell her and was sent staggering by a blow to the head. A rock as big as a melon thudded to the earth at his feet. His sense reeling, he sagged against the wall and rasped, "Watch what the hell you're doing."

"I'm watching just fine."

Fargo glanced up. She was on her knees above the trapdoor, holding another huge rock.

"Thanks for your help," Esther said, and let go.

Fargo dived flat. The rock hit him on the shoulder, lancing pain clear down to his hips. He rolled and swung the Henry toward the opening just as more dirt showered down. He couldn't see for all the dust. Shaking his head to clear it, he made it to his knees.

Above him, the trapdoor slammed shut.

Fargo clutched at the ladder and pulled himself to his feet. Blood was trickling down his face from a gash over his temple. He was lucky she hadn't crushed his skull.

Fargo went up the ladder. He pressed with all his might but the trapdoor wouldn't move. Scritching and scratching noises puzzled him until he realized she was piling rocks and dirt on top of it. She had sealed him in.

Fargo swore. She had played him for a jackass. It wasn't hard to guess why. He knew too much. She wanted to get rid of him so he couldn't report her to the law. Not that he would but she didn't know that.

Left with no choice, Fargo climbed down. The bleeding was worse so he untied his bandanna and mopped at the blood. From overhead came mocking laughter.

"Can you hear me down there? I want to thank you for making it so easy. I suppose I could have shot you but I like this way better. Now you and that monster can kill each other off." Esther's laughter trailed off into the night.

Fargo continued on. There were more trapdoors and he would find one.

It wasn't long before he came to another junction. The new tunnel, if his sense of direction wasn't off, led toward Kill Creek. He took it.

No sounds reached him, either from ahead or behind. For the moment he was safe.

Fargo never had liked being taken advantage of, and he wasn't one to turn the other cheek. He didn't do unto others as he wanted them to do to him. Hurt him once and he never forgot and never forgave. He had several scores to settle now, and he wasn't leaving Kill Creek until he did.

Deep in thought, Fargo almost missed an opening in the left wall.

It was another chamber. He entered and felt along the wall and nearly yipped with glee when his questing fingers found a lantern on a peg. He lit it and raised it over his head.

The walls were solid rock laced with quartz. Someone had been at the quartz with a pick and left large piles. Flashes of yellow drew Fargo to the nearest. He picked up a chunk and held it to the lantern. He wasn't an expert but he was willing to bet the yellow was fool's gold. Whoever did the chipping had gone to a lot of trouble for nothing.

Fargo moved on. He was tired of being underground. He wasn't one of those who couldn't abide tight spaces but he wasn't a mole, either. He walked faster now that he had light, alert for another ladder.

The tunnel forked. He took the right branch but it went only sixty feet and ended at a dirt wall. He turned to go back.

At the limit of the light, something moved.

Instantly, Fargo raised the Henry.

Whatever or whoever it was didn't come closer.

"Who's there?" Fargo demanded. He wasn't expecting an answer but he got one in the form of a growl. Only the growl didn't sound as if it came from a mastiff or some other animal. The throat that made it was human.

Fargo sighted down the barrel. He took a few steps and the shape retreated. "You're Maxine's pa, aren't you?"

Another growl was the answer.

"I don't scare easy," Fargo said. When he still got no reply, he angrily snapped, "Talk to me, you son of a bitch."

"Thief," the shape rumbled.

"What?"

"You try take treasure."

"What treasure? That fool's gold?"

"You the fool," the shape said, and melted away.

Fargo broke into a run, his boots slapping the earth. Up ahead, other boots did the same. He ran faster, the lantern swinging wildly. He caught sight of the brown robe or frock or whatever it was. "Stop!"

His quarry was a two-legged antelope.

Fargo was so intent on catching up that he didn't look down. He didn't notice that the dirt had been disturbed, or that a part of the tunnel floor wasn't dirt at all. It was canvas covered with dirt. Only when he took another stride and the canvas gave way did he awaken to his peril. He tried to fling himself back but his momentum did him in. Down he pitched, headlong to the bottom. The impact knocked the breath from his lungs. The lantern crashed and broke and he was mired in ink.

He had blundered again but his other blunders were nothing compared to this one.

He had fallen into a pit.

14

Fargo's shoulder and side throbbed. He propped himself on his other arm and flexed his shoulder and raised and lowered his arm a few times to see if anything was broken. In the pitch-black it was impossible to tell how deep the pit was. He guessed about ten feet. Sitting up, he felt the ground around him for the Henry. A sharp sting in his middle finger caused him to jerk his hand back. He had cut himself on a piece of broken glass from the lantern.

More carefully now, Fargo ran both hands over the bottom. He found the Henry, and stood. Backing against the pit wall, he placed one boot in front of the other until he came to the other end. The pit was twelve feet long. He did the same from side to side and measured the same.

From above came a guttural laugh.

Fargo glanced up. Crouched on the lip was a hulking form. "Come back to gloat?"

A voice that brought to mind the rumbling of a bear answered with, "Brom trick you."

"That's your name? Brom?"

"Bromley. Everybody call me Brom."

"You're Maxine's and Serilda's pa."

"Brom's girls. Good girls. But Serilda not always listen. She too nice, that one."

Fargo wasn't the only one who had blundered. He started to raise the Henry to his sore shoulder.

"Don't," Brom warned. "Make Brom mad, Brom kill quick."

Fargo was taken aback. "You can see in the dark?"

"Brom like cat. Live down here many years. See good."

"Why the hell do you talk like that?"

"Like what?"

"Like you're two years old." Fargo was stalling. He needed to learn as much as he could. Maybe, just maybe, he could talk his way out.

"You poke fun at Brom?"

"I just want to know."

The hulk was quiet a bit, then rumbled, "Brom show you. Brom be back." His silhouette vanished.

Fargo roved the pit walls. He jumped up a few times but couldn't reach the top. He had completed a circuit and was back where he started when without any sound whatsoever, his captor was back.

"Put rifle on ground."

Fargo did as he was bid.

"Pistol too."

"Why?"

"Brom not stupid. You want answer, you put pistol on ground with rifle."

Fargo reckoned he had nothing to lose. He slicked the Colt out and set it down, then held his hands out from his sides. "Happy now? Suppose you tell me what this is all about."

"First show," Brom said.

Light flared. Fargo blinked against the glare and squinted up. "What is it you want to show me?"

Brom was holding a lantern in a gnarled hand. He placed it next to him, reached up, and pulled back his hood.

Fargo couldn't help himself; he recoiled a step.

"Brom handsome, yes?"

Fargo was speechless. No wonder Esther had called him a monster. Bromley's head was a misshapen ruin. The left half was normal except for the left eye, which bulged obscenely. It was the right half that was hideous. Nearly bald save for scraggily tufts, the skull had partially caved in and the ear was split in half. The right cheek was twice the size of the left, and the right eye bulged even more than its counterpart. As if that weren't enough, the corner of the man's mouth drooped and oozed drool. His neck, thick as a bull's and corded with muscle, was oddly bent so he couldn't hold his head straight.

"Brom handsome, yes?"

"What happened to you?"

Brom touched his misshapen face. "Beam fall on Brom. Brom nearly die. When Brom better, he look like this. Now Brom ugly. No one like to look at him. Not even own girls. Brom scare them."

"That's why you wear the robe and hood."

Brom plucked at the folds. "This belong to priest once. Him like you, a thief. He wanted Brom's treasure. Brom not let him have it."

"You killed him?"

"Wring his neck like this." Brom mimicked strangling someone and then ripping their head from their shoulders. "Priest flop like chicken. Brom take robe so not scare girls."

"What was that about treasure?"

"You saw. You know. It is why you here."

"That's fool's gold. It's worthless."

"You try fool Brom. It not work."

"I'm not after your gold or anything else," Fargo sought to set him straight.

"Liar!" Brom roared, his ravaged features coloring red. "You the same as everybody else. You want what is Brom's."

"Listen to me . . ." Fargo said, but the ravaged madman paid him no mind.

"This place Brom's. Treasure Brom's. Brom not let you have it. Brom not let others have it. Brom kill you all. Even one who say he wanted Brom's help."

"Who was that?"

Brom smiled a lopsided smile. "That all Brom tell." He

pulled his hood up, and stood. "You die slow, thief. No food. No water. Take days, maybe."

"I'll give you one last chance," Fargo said. "Get me out of this and let me take the blond woman with me and you can do whatever the hell you want to the others."

"You like blond woman, yes?"

"She's a friend. So what do you say?"

Brom leaned down and with vicious spite declared, "Brom say he bring her to you. Brom say you and her die together." With that, he strode off.

Fargo lunged for the Colt. As quick as he was, he had no one to shoot. Mocking mirth filled the tunnel. Fargo shoved the Colt into his holster and picked up the Henry. He had learned enough to know that he was dealing with a lunatic. The accident had done something to the man's mind. Warped it, twisted it as the beam had twisted Brom's face.

A shadow flitted across the pit.

Fargo looked up, thinking Brom had come back but it was only a moth fluttering about the lantern. The madman hadn't bothered to take it with him. Another blunder on Brom's part.

Fargo inspected the pit walls. They were sheer and hard packed. He sprang for the rim but fell short.

Holding the Henry by the barrel and the stock, Fargo threw it up and beyond the lantern, an easy toss that shouldn't damage it any. Then he backed to the far end and crouched. Coiling his legs, he exploded into motion. Three bounds carried him the entire length. He launched himself into the air, his arms extended. His fingers caught the edge but he couldn't hold on. With an oath he fell to the bottom, alighting on the balls of his feet.

"Damn."

Fargo drew the Arkansas toothpick. At waist height he dug a foothold wide enough for the toe of his boot to fit. Wiping the blade clean on his buckskins, he slid the toothpick into his ankle sheath and once again moved to the other end. Once again he crouched. Once again he coiled. He must time it just right. If he missed, or if his boot wedged too tight, he might break a toe or his ankle or even his leg.

Three bounds, and Fargo sprang. He jammed his boot into the foothold and levered higher, his arms as far over his head as he could reach. The extra boost did the trick. His forearms shot over the rim. Digging his elbows in, he held fast and pumped his legs. His knee bumped the lantern and it started to go over the side but he caught hold of the handle.

Fargo grinned. He had done it. He gazed down into the pit and noticed something he hadn't noticed earlier. It explained how Brom had made it past the pit without falling in. On the left the pit was flush with the tunnel wall but on the right there was a lip just wide enough for a man to cross if he was careful.

Retrieving the Henry, Fargo ran. He came to a fork and bore to the right and presently came on another and this time went straight. By his reckoning he should be directly under Kill Creek.

A ladder appeared. Setting the lantern down, Fargo climbed. He tried the trapdoor and it swung up without protest. He was in an empty room. From beyond came muffled voices. Clambering out, he quietly lowered the trapdoor.

The room was familiar. He was in the back of the saloon. He crept to the door and cracked it open. The voices were louder but not loud enough that he could hear what they were saying. Slipping out, he glided along the hall until he was almost to the light.

"—hear another word out of you," Moon grated. "You can't blame me for what happened."

"Like hell we can't." This from Tucker.

Fargo flattened. They were just around the corner.

"You said you had it worked out," Tucker continued. "You said they'd do as you wanted. But now Shorty's dead and one of us could be next. Beck and me are for lighting a shuck, and I don't mean tomorrow."

"You're siding with him?" Moon asked.

"Everything has gone to hell," Beck replied. "We can't trust them anymore, if we ever could."

"All that money. We're supposed to ride off and forget it?"

Tucker answered. "We can't spend any if we're maggot bait. And I don't mind admitting that that loco son of a bitch scares the hell out of me."

"Conklin, where do you stand?" Moon said.

"With you, like always."

"Then it's two against two."

"No one is against anyone," Tucker said. "We just don't think it's smart to stick with a losing hand."

"He's not bulletproof. We shoot him, he'll die, the same as you or me."

"But how many of us will he do in before we bring him down? He's not human. Those dandies are one thing; that damned lunatic another."

"And then there's that redhead and her dogs," Beck said. "She'll try to stop us if she finds out."

"She'll listen to me. I can talk her into anything."

Tucker snorted. "You talked her into this and look at where it's got us. She's almost as loco as her pa."

"Be careful."

"Don't get mad. I'm only saying, is all. It'll be days before the money gets here. A lot can happen, and none of it good."

"Half a million dollars," Moon said.

"It's not worth dying for."

"Half a million dollars split four ways is one hundred and twenty-five thousand dollars."

"Each?" Beck said.

"Each and every one of us."

"Hell," Beck said. "I didn't realize it was that much. I wouldn't need to work the rest of my born days."

"Don't listen to him," Tucker urged.

"You heard him," Beck said. "One hundred and twenty-five thousand dollars *each*."

"Remember Shorty's head," Tucker said.

"Shorty was careless," Moon declared. "We won't be. The four of us will stick together so he can't jump us. He tries anything, he's dead and we're rich."

"You're forgetting the bitch and the blonde," Conklin broke his long silence.

"I'm not forgetting anyone. We already agreed what to do about them and the dandies."

"Not the city gals. I mean your redhead and her sister. Beck is right. They're awful protective of that pa of theirs."

"I don't care . . ." Moon began, and stopped at a yell from down the street.

"Listen."

Fargo heard it, too. James Harker, shouting for Moon and his men.

"What the hell does he want now?" Tucker rasped. "I'm sick to death of that no account. I'd as soon blow his brains out as look at him."

"When the time comes, he's mine," Moon said. "I want him to crawl. I want him to beg. Him and his airs. I'll teach him."

The light and their voices dwindled. The saloon fell quiet and dark.

Fargo stood. From what he'd gathered, there was a lot more to this than he thought. Exactly how all the pieces of the puzzle fit was still a mystery. Not that he cared. His sole aim now was to whisk Gretchen out of Kill Creek, and Serilda if she wanted to come, and leave the rest to do themselves in as they saw fit.

Fargo went to the batwing, took off his hat, and poked his head out. The four lead chuckers were passing the butcher shop. Farther down, the Ovaro was still tied to the post. "Hang on, big fella," Fargo said out loud. "We're leaving this ghost town in two shakes of a lamb's tail."

"That's what you think."

Fargo spun.

Maxine had come out of the hall and was holding a revolver on him. "Miss me, handsome?"

"I met your pa."

"Did you, now? And you're still alive? I can remedy that."

"It doesn't have to be like this," Fargo said.

Maxine took a step and tossed her wild mane of hair. "Sure it does. You killed one of my dogs, you son of a bitch."

"It was him or me."

"Well, now it's your turn," Maxine said, and raised the revolver.

15

Fargo threw himself under the batwing as the boom of her six-shooter filled the saloon. The slug bit into the jamb and sent slivers flying. He rolled to the left and was up and to the corner before she could shoot again. He drew his Colt and covered the doorway.

Down the street, Moon's bunch had heard the blast and were hurrying back.

Fargo turned and ran to the rear of the saloon and along the backs of the buildings until he came to the house he was looking for. Darting between it and the next, he jogged to the front.

The Ovaro was only a few yards away but it wasn't alone.

James and Landreth were nearby, staring down the street.

"What do you suppose that shot was about?" the former wondered.

"There's no telling. Moon and his goons went into the saloon and now it's gone quiet. Maybe we should go see."

"And leave the ladies unprotected?" James objected. "I should say not. From now on we don't leave their sides."

"We can take them with us."

James hesitated. "I suppose that's better than standing here not knowing. From what Esther told us, the madman who took her is quite fierce. Moon and his men could be dead for all we know."

"At least we're rid of the scout," Landreth mentioned. "I never did like him."

"I wasn't all that fond of him either but I wouldn't want to die the way he did." James shuddered. "Buried alive, Esther said, when part of a tunnel collapsed on top of him. She was lucky to make it out alive."

Just then the door opened and out came the woman who had tried to take Fargo's life. She wore a dress and had cleaned herself up and was holding a lantern.

"Was that a gunshot I heard a minute ago?"

"Yes, dear. Down near the saloon." James took the lantern. "Moon went to investigate and hasn't come out."

"Where's Gretchen?" Landreth asked.

"She says she is staying in our room until morning," Esther said. "She's been cross with me ever since I escaped from that monster. I suspect it has something to do with Fargo. She was very fond of him."

"Yet another reason I'm glad he's dead," Landreth declared.

Esther stared down the street. "We should go see about Mr. Moon. If that brute and his girls have killed them, we need to know."

"What about Gretchen?" James said. "We can't leave her here alone no matter what she wants."

Esther motioned. "Frankly, I don't give a damn. I was flattered when she insisted on coming along to be sure I was safe but she's turned out to be more of a bother than she's worth. I particularly don't like that she cozied up to Fargo after I explicitly told her not to." Esther took his arm. "Come on."

Landreth glanced at the millinery and frowned but he went with them.

Fargo smiled. He waited until they were well along, then ran to the dress shop and ducked inside. The door to the bedroom was shut so he knocked.

"Who is it?" Gretchen demanded.

Fargo told her.

There was a squeal of delight and the door was flung wide

and Gretchen threw herself at him and hugged him close, saying in his ear, "Thank God. Esther told us you were dead."

"I almost was, thanks to her." Fargo took Gretchen's hand. "We're getting out of here."

"But my things . . ."

"What's more important, your clothes or your life?" Fargo pulled and she came with him. The street was temporarily empty. Quickly stepping to the Ovaro, he untied the reins and swung up. "Grab hold," he said, and offered his arm.

Gretchen wrapped her arms around his middle and rested her cheek on his back. "I'm so happy you're alive."

"Makes two of us." Fargo reined toward the bluffs. He rode at a walk until he was sure he was out of earshot. At a trot he looped around until he came to the old road, well past Kill Creek. A dark wall of forest hemmed both sides. From its depths issued shrieks and bays and an occasional roar.

They had gone a quarter of a mile when Gretchen straightened and said quietly, "I can't."

"Can't what?"

"Leave Esther this way. It's not right. You have to take me back."

"Like hell."

"She's my friend. I can't up and abandon her, even if we have had a spat."

Fargo told her what he'd overheard, adding, "If she doesn't care about you, you shouldn't give a damn about her."

"That was her anger talking. Deep down Esther cares for me. I know she does. I can't desert her. I wouldn't be able to live with myself."

"I'm not turning back." As far as Fargo was concerned, the rest could kill themselves off, and good riddance. He liked Serilda, but when she threw that dirt in his face and ran off, she had made it plain where her sentiments lay.

"Please."

"No, damn it. Don't ask again."

"You owe me this favor."

112

Fargo swore. Women everywhere were the same. Make love to a female and she considered the man to be in her debt for as long as he drew breath.

Gretchen had more to say. "You won't want to hear this but you have a streak of decency in you or I would never have let you have me. I'm appealing to that streak. If it was your best friend back there, you wouldn't run out on them."

"You don't know me," Fargo said gruffly.

Gretchen reached around and touched his cheek. "I know what my heart tells me and my heart never lies."

"Women and their hearts."

"Men and their stubborn streaks," Gretchen retorted. "I know I'm right. Why else did you come to get me? Please. I'm begging you. Turn around."

Fargo cursed some more, then drew rein and shifted in the saddle. "We're shed of that place. We got away clean and we should keep on going. We'll head for the nearest town and look up the law and have them deal with it."

"By then Esther could be dead." Gretchen shook her head. "No. If you won't turn back, I'll go alone."

"Damn you."

"You don't mean that." Gretchen put her hands on the saddle and went to push off.

Fargo grabbed her wrist. "Hold on. You win. But we should wait until daylight."

"No."

"Esther will be all right until then. James and Landreth are there to protect her." The truth was, Fargo doubted the pair could fend off a riled chipmunk but he kept that to himself.

"I don't know," Gretchen said uncertainly.

"If we hear a shot or a scream we'll head back," Fargo promised.

"I suppose it would be all right. We haven't gone all that far."

Fargo reined into the trees and came on a small clearing.

He helped her down, then proceeded to untie his bedroll and spread it out for her to sit on. He opened a saddlebag, took out his pemmican, and offered her a piece.

"What's this?"

"Ground buffalo meat mixed with fat and chokecherries. I got it from a Shoshone gal."

"Buffalo meat and fat?" Gretchen shoved it at him. "No thank you. I've never eaten buffalo meat and fat doesn't appeal to me."

Fargo didn't take it. He sat next to her, selected a piece for himself, and bit off the end. Chewing lustily, he smacked his lips. "You don't know what you're missing. Pemmican has jerky beat all hollow."

Gretchen watched him chew. Scowling, she took a tentative nibble, chewed a while, and smiled. "You know, it's not half bad. I should thank you for going to so much trouble on my behalf. You've been more of a gentleman than James and Roy put together."

To the north a ululating cry rose on the wind.

Gretchen's head snapped up and she looked fearfully about her. "Did you hear that?"

"It was a wolf and wolves don't bother people much," Fargo enlightened her. "You're safe."

As if to prove him wrong, the screech of a mountain lion echoed off a high slope.

"Safe, you say?" Gretchen moved closer. "I don't mind admitting the wilds frighten me, and always have. I don't know how you do what you do."

Fargo shrugged. "We get used to things."

"Used to bears out to rend you limb from limb? Or painted hostiles out to lift your hair? I could never get used to that."

"It's not as if I run into a griz every other day."

"Once a lifetime is enough for me." Gretchen regarded him thoughtfully. "You're a rare breed, Skye, whether you're willing to admit it or not."

Fargo was never comfortable talking about himself. He changed the subject.

"Are you going to report her when you get back to civilization?"

"Esther?"

"No. The queen of England."

"Haven't you been listening? Esther is my best friend. I could no more report her than I could abandon her."

"She doesn't feel the same about you."

"Be that as it may," Gretchen persisted, "I have been her friend for too many years to turn my back on her when she needs me most. So no, if I make it back, I'm not going to turn her in. I hope she and James make it to Paris and live happily ever after."

"There's no such thing."

"Don't you have a shred of romance in your soul? Everything Esther has done, she's done out of love. I might not agree with how she has gone about it but I admire her devotion to her man."

"You don't care that she's going to steal half a million dollars from her own pa?"

"Her father can afford it."

"That's no answer."

Gretchen was about to take another bite of pemmican but lowered it. "I'm not perfect. I have faults the same as everybody else. One of them is loyalty to my friends, no matter what they do."

Fargo admired her for that. He was about to say so when the crack of a twig brought him to his feet, his right hand on the Colt.

Gretchen stood up too. "What was that?" She sidled over and her arm touched his. "Some kind of animal?"

"A deer, maybe," Fargo said to set her at ease. The vegetation was a patchwork of dark shapes and sizes, any one of which could be responsible.

"Or a bear," Gretchen said fearfully.

"Bears usually make a lot more noise."

"Usually?"

As Fargo could have told her, when a bear wanted to it could move as silently as a ghost. Another tidbit he kept to himself.

"We should build a fire. Fires keep animals away."

"They would see it in Kill Creek."

"Then we should find a spot where we can build one that they can't see. I'd sleep better."

Fargo thought he saw something move and focused on the spot but nothing appeared.

"In fact, why don't we roll up your blankets and leave right this minute?" Gretchen suggested.

The Ovaro suddenly nickered and stamped a hoof.

Fargo drew his Colt. "Get behind me."

"What is it?"

"I don't know yet."

The stallion had its ear up and was staring into the woods near where Fargo had spotted movement. So something *was* out there. He thumbed back the Colt's hammer.

"Maybe it will leave us be," Gretchen said.

"Maybe." It had been Fargo's experience that nine times out of ten, meat-eaters fought shy of people. It was that tenth time a person had to worry about.

"I sure hope you're right about it being a deer."

Fargo wished she would stop talking. He spied a patch of black that did not appear to be part of the surrounding brush. "Stay here." He took a step and she gripped his wrist.

"No, you don't."

"I'll be right back."

"Then where you go, I go."

Rather than argue, Fargo moved toward the edge of the clearing. She held his arm so tight, her nails dug into his skin. "You're fretting over nothing," he said.

From the depths of a thicket came a growl.

"I knew it!" Gretchen cried.

"Get behind me," Fargo urged. He tried to tug his arm free but she wouldn't let go.

There was another growl, and the undergrowth crackled, and the next moment, the creature stalked into view.

"Dear God," Gretchen said. "How did it find us?"

"Its nose," Fargo guessed.

The mastiff crouched to spring.

16

Fargo's first thought was that where there was one mastiff there were bound to be the others. "Get behind me," he said again, and raised the Colt.

Gretchen was rooted in place, her hands clamped on his arm. "Look at how big it is."

Fargo was well aware of its size. He must make his first shot count or it would be on them ripping and rending. He aimed at the center of the dark rectangle that was its head. "Watch for the other two."

"Where?" Gretchen exclaimed, and whirled. In doing so, she didn't let go, and when she turned, she jerked him half around.

The mastiff snarled and attacked.

Fargo fired and missed. He thumbed back the hammer to shoot again but the dog was a fluid streak and already on them. It leaped as he squeezed the trigger.

The impact knocked him back. He tripped over Gretchen and went down with the mastiff on top. Its fangs snapped at his jugular. Letting go of the Colt, he grabbed its throat and tried to force it back.

Growling savagely, the dog snapped and gnashed.

Spittle flecked Fargo's face. He exerted all his strength but those slavering fangs came closer. The dog's eyes seemed to glow with preternatural hellfire. He thrust his legs up to kick it off but the animal was too heavy. All he did was provoke it into a frenzy.

"My Colt!" Fargo shouted. "Shoot it!" He couldn't see Gretchen and couldn't take his eyes off the mastiff to see if she was still there or had run off.

He didn't take her for a coward but her fear might have gotten the better of her.

The dog lunged, and Fargo almost lost his hold. Its teeth came within a whisker of sinking into his neck. He shoved but it was like trying to push a boulder.

"Shoot it!"

Fargo kept thinking about the other two dogs. They were bound to show up and if all three attacked him at once when he was on the ground like this, the outcome was a foregone conclusion.

The mastiff flailed it paws, clawing at his buckskins, at his chest.

Fargo changed tactics. He flung both legs wide and wrapped them around the dog's body. Then, firming his hold on its neck, he threw all his weight into rolling. He got the dog on its side but he wasn't any better off than before. Its fangs were still dangerously near his throat. He didn't dare slacken his grip.

Fargo dug his fingers in as deep as they would go. If he couldn't let go he would strangle the son of a bitch. But its neck was so thick and so corded with muscle that it was like trying to strangle a log. To make matters worse, he was tiring. Yet the dog was as strong and determined as ever, a churning, raging engine of destruction that wouldn't be denied.

Of all the ways Fargo thought he might die, being killed by a dog wasn't one of them. He pushed and rolled again and succeeded in flipping the dog onto its back so that now he was on top. He pressed down, his thumbs steel spikes.

The mastiff went berserk.

Fargo's hold slipped. Another few seconds and the beast would break free. Suddenly the Colt was in front of his eyes. The muzzle jammed against the dog's head and the six-gun went off. The flash and the thunder sent his senses spinning.

The mastiff yelped and went limp. Its legs stopping thrashing and its tongue lolled from a mouth gone slack.

Overcome by weariness, Fargo slowly released his hold and rose onto his knees. He shook its head to be sure it was dead.

Gretchen crouched next to him, the smoking Colt in her hand. "Is it . . . ?" she fearfully asked.

"It is," Fargo confirmed, and had to add, "Took you long enough."

"I'm sorry. I couldn't find your revolver. It went flying when you fell." Gretchen held out her arm. "Look at me. I'm shaking like a leaf."

Fargo grunted and sat back. His buckskins were torn and he was bleeding.

"Hell."

"Let me see."

"The other dogs," Fargo reminded her, and took the Colt. He scanned the clearing but they still hadn't appeared.

"I haven't seen any others."

Fargo didn't understand. The mastiffs always traveled together. Or had this one picked up the Ovaro's scent and trailed them on its own? Involuntarily, he shivered. He was cold and clammy and not just from his sweat but also from the blood he could feel trickling from the cuts. "I reckon he was alone."

Gretchen raised his shirt and touched a slash. "I need to wash your wounds."

"They aren't that deep."

"Infection might set in."

The nearest water was the stream by the bluff. Fargo was loathe to go out in the open but she was right. "Damn it to hell."

"You sure do swear a lot."

Fargo chuckled. She should hear him when he was really mad. Rising, he replaced the spent cartridge. Together they rolled up his blankets and moved to the Ovaro. The stallion hadn't run off as a lot of horses would have done. It was uncommonly devoted and dependable, yet another reason Fargo valued his mount above all else.

Out on the road the wind was stronger and brought with it the feral chorus of fang and claw.

Fargo reined toward Kill Creek. Gretchen pressed against him, her warmth welcome, her hands on his shoulders.

"You were marvelous back there."

"I was lucky."

"We're still going back in the morning, aren't we?"

"I said we would."

"Don't be mad. Maybe she isn't as good a friend to me as I am to her but that's her and not me. And she wasn't always this way. When we were little we were inseparable. More like sisters than friends. We played together and ate together and she even helped nurse me when I was sick. You can't expect me to turn my back on her when she needs me most."

"She's not little anymore."

"You're saying she's changed? I suppose you're right. I have seen a difference the past few years. But she's still very much the girl I grew up with. I can no more abandon her than you could your horse."

"What made you say that?"

"I saw how upset you were when it was taken. You would kill for this animal, wouldn't you?"

"Damn right I would."

"There you have it. End of discussion."

Fargo refused to give up. "You go back, you could wind up dead."

"I'm not stupid."

"I could wind up dead too."

"You don't have to go with me. You're under no obligation."

"Except to myself."

"How do you mean?"

"I have some scores to settle." The list was as long as

121

Fargo's arm. He'd been shot at. He'd been clubbed. He'd had dogs set on him. He'd had rocks dropped on his head and been caught in a pit, and as she just mentioned, he'd had his horse taken. An eye for an eye was his code. He'd been willing to put it off in order to get Gretchen to safety, but now that she wanted to return, it was time for him to start doing unto others as they kept doing unto him.

The bluffs towered like black monoliths. Fargo drew rein at a gravel bar and helped Gretchen down. Sliding from the saddle, he set his hat next to him, stripped off his buckskin shirt, and dipped a hand in the water.

"Let me." Gretchen hiked her dress and ripped a strip from the hem. Wadding it, she soaked it, then commenced washing the claw marks and scrapes. "It would help if I had a fire to see by."

"We're too close to Kill Creek."

"We could find a spot where they can't see."

"Here is fine." Fargo liked the spot. They had the bluffs to one side and a low hummock on the other.

Gretchen leaned closer. "It's hard to see." She dabbed at a cut high on his chest, her breath warm on his skin. "I hope this doesn't hurt."

It occurred to Fargo that they had the rest of the night to themselves and he wasn't the least bit sleepy. He kissed her on the forehead.

"What was that for?"

"Guess."

Gretchen stopped wiping and said in amazement, "You can't be thinking what I think you're thinking."

"Why not?"

"We're out in the open in the middle of the wilds in the dark of night. Anything or anyone could happen by at any time."

Fargo patted the Colt. "Let them."

"Be serious."

Fargo kissed her on the mouth. "I am."

"No."

Fargo ran a hand from her wrist to her elbow to her shoulder. He rubbed her neck and traced her ear with his fingertip. She gave a slight shudder.

"Didn't you hear me?"

"My ears work fine. So does the rest of me."

"But you're hurt."

"Not where it counts." Cupping her chin, Fargo let the next kiss linger. When he drew back she poked him in the chest.

"When I said no I meant it. I'm not about to do *that* here. The idea is preposterous."

Fargo placed his right hand and on her breast and massaged it through her dress. She grabbed his wrist as if to pull his hand away, but didn't. Her nipples hardened like nails, and he smiled. "Like that, do you?"

"I should beat you with a rock."

"What's stopping you?"

"When a lady says she's not interested, you should respect her wishes," Gretchen said softly.

"The lady in you might not want to," Fargo said, "but the woman in you does."

"They are one and the same."

Fargo cupped her other breast and squeezed both, hard. She arched her back and moaned. "Which was that? The lady or the woman?"

"Give me a rock."

Pulling her to him, Fargo kissed her fiercely while kneading and pinching her mounds. This time when he drew back, she was panting.

"You are the most stubborn man who ever drew breath."

Fargo rose and she stood with him. He sculpted his hands to her rounded bottom and ground against her while kissing her neck and ear.

"You're infuriating."

Sliding a hand between her thighs, Fargo fondled her nether

mount. She was a furnace, and when he rubbed, she gasped and dug her nails into his arms.

"God help me, I love it!"

"Was that the lady talking or the woman?"

"Enough. I get your point."

With a deft dip of his knees, Fargo scooped her into his arms, carried her to the grassy hummock, and laid her on her back. Starlight lent her face a lovely luster and her hair was a corn silk halo. He sank down and put his hand on her belly. Under his palm, she quivered. "Still want me to stop?"

"Brute."

Fargo stretched full length beside her. He rubbed in small circles from her stomach to her cleavage and began to undo her buttons and stays.

"You're going too slow."

"We have all night."

"I want it now." Gretchen brazenly reached down and folded her fingers over his engorged member. "You only have yourself to blame." She stroked him, and grinned. "My oh my. It appears you want it as much as I do."

"Brute," Fargo said.

Gretchen laughed. "Nothing else to say?"

Fargo fused his mouth and his body to hers. The chill of the night wind gave way to the warmth of her luscious body. She squirmed and mewed and nipped his chin with her teeth.

"You have no idea what you do to me."

Fargo begged to differ, but didn't. He kissed and licked and fondled. Soon she was mashing her breasts into his chest and her hips into his. He got his pants down around his knees and her dress hiked around her waist. Pulsing with need, he knelt between her legs.

"Please," Gretchen said.

It was the millinery all over again, only now Fargo could take his time and pace himself. She was drenched and quivering as he penetrated. Her velvet sheath rippling, she wrapped her legs around him.

"Now?"

"Now," Fargo said.

Afterward they lay side by side, her head on his shoulder. She twirled his hair and moved her palm over his beard.

"When I'm with you, I feel as if I'm floating on a cloud. Why is that?"

"Do you float before or after you gush?"

"You are a cad, sir," Gretchen said playfully.

Fargo closed his eyes. He was drowsy and wouldn't mind sleeping a spell. He suggested the same to her.

"I'm not tired. I was until you had your way with me. Now I'm bubbling with energy. You would think it would be the opposite." She pecked his cheek. "You must be magic."

Behind Fargo someone snickered. "For his next trick he can try rising from the dead."

17

Fargo had set his Colt beside him when he undid his pants. The instant he heard the voice, he lunged for it, only it wasn't there. Looking up, he beheld Tucker and Beck. Both held leveled six-shooters. Tucker also had the Colt.

"Looking for this? You were having so much fun with the lady, I snuck right up and took it."

Fargo was furious. Not at them, at himself. His lust had made him careless.

Beck said, "We were nice and polite and let you finish." He cackled. "You sure did give it to her good."

"I'll say," Tucker agreed. "It made me want to do her my own self but Moon would put windows in my skull."

"Damn him, anyway," Beck said.

Tucker gestured. "Hitch up those buckskin britches of yours. And Miss Worth, you do yourself up. Do it quick, too. We've been away too long as it is."

Fargo had to ask. "How in hell did you find us?" It was impossible for them to have tracked him in the dark, not without torches. Besides which, they didn't impress him as being able to track a bull buffalo in mud.

"The dog the redhead sent on your trail," Tucker said. "We were supposed to follow it right to you but the stupid thing went and ran on ahead and we lost it. We were talking over what to do when we heard you coming back down the road so we hid and then came after you."

"Pretty clever, huh?" Beck boasted.

Fargo rose to his knees and pulled up his pants. "Maxine and you are working together?"

"Not us," Tucker said. "She's Moon's. Either of us so much as looks at her wrong, he's liable to put slugs in us."

"Damn him, anyway," Beck said again.

Fargo was trying to make sense of it all but a few pieces to the puzzle were missing. "Moon and Maxine? How long has that been going on?"

"Oh, hell," Tucker said. "A year or more, I reckon."

"We were running from the law," Beck took up the account, "and we stopped in Kill Creek for the night. We figured it was deserted, being a ghost town and all. We didn't know about that loco Bromley living down in the tunnels with his girls. Maxine showed herself, and Moon took a fancy to her. They've been close ever since."

"The lucky bastard," Tucker said. "She's a looker, that gal. But looks ain't everything. Takes after her pa in that she's half loco herself."

Gretchen was swiftly dressing but she stopped to say, "Does all this have anything to do with why Mr. Moon suggested we come to Kill Creek to wait for the money?"

"Of course it does, you stupid cow," Tucker replied. "Did you really think we'd settle for fifty thousand when there's half a million to be had?"

"I'm not sure I understand."

Beck snorted. "Got to spell it out for you, do we? Moon brought you here to dispose of you once the money comes. He figured to let that crazy Bromley do you in. That way the lunatic would be blamed and not us."

"Maxine promised she could keep her pa under control until Moon wanted it done," Tucker said bitterly, "but then the crazy bastard went and bashed poor Shorty's brains out. I could have told Moon we couldn't trust that loon but he wouldn't listen."

"You're despicable," Gretchen said.

"Don't get on your high horse with us, bitch," Beck snapped. "We know James Harker hired us so the law would blame us for taking you ladies and not him and that Roy. We know James and Roy planned to shoot us and leave our bodies for the law to find to give the law the notion we had a falling-out over the money."

"Which no one would ever find," Tucker said.

"James never said anything about that to me."

"Why should he, lady? From what I can gather, you're the only one of them who is halfway decent. That Esther? The one you think is your friend? You ought to ask her what she plans to do to you."

"Tell me."

Tucker shook his head. "You won't believe it, coming from me. Moon heard her and James talking one night and told us."

Fargo had most of it now. They were a bunch of vipers, with betrayal piled on betrayal. He fastened his belt and reached down as if to adjust his pant leg and slid his fingers into his boot. Neither Tucker nor Beck noticed.

"Hurry it up, lady," the latter said to Gretchen. "Moon is expecting us to fetch you back."

"As for you," Tucker smirked at Fargo. "That dog was supposed to do you in but I reckon you must have done him. Now we'll have to do you our own selves."

Fargo was ready. "What about the other two dogs?"

"Which?" Tucker said.

Fargo pointed behind them. "Those two yonder. Did Maxine send them along too?"

It worked beautifully. Both gun sharks looked over their shoulders.

Fargo streaked up and in and buried the Arkansas toothpick to the hilt in Tucker's neck. Without slowing he twisted and thrust at Beck but Beck yelped and scrambled back and his revolver went off, the slug kicking dirt next to Fargo's leg. Fargo was on him in a bound and grabbed Beck's wrist but Beck was able to grab his. They struggled, arms and legs straining, Beck seeking to point his revolver, Fargo to wrench free and use the toothpick. Beck kicked at Fargo's knee and Fargo sidestepped and Beck's other foot hooked him and down Fargo went with Beck on his chest.

"Bastard," Beck hissed, his wrist slowly turning, the muzzle slowly swinging toward Fargo's face.

Fargo heaved but Beck clung on. Fargo rammed a knee up but all Beck did was grunt. He went to slam his forehead into Beck's face when suddenly the barrel of a six-gun was pressed against the side of Beck's head. Beck started to jerk away just as the revolver went off.

Blood and gore splattered Fargo. He instinctively closed his eyes. His ears ringing, he shoved the body off, sat up, and wiped his sleeve across his face. "I'm obliged." When Gretchen didn't respond, he looked up.

She was staring aghast at the body. "I did it again, only this time it was a human being."

"You sure as hell did."

"I've never . . ." Gretchen let the revolver drop, and shuddered. "Oh, God. What have I done?"

Fargo stood and enfolded her in his arms. "Don't be so hard on yourself. You did it to save my hide."

"I saw the gun and I wasn't thinking and I grabbed it. . . ." Gretchen sobbed. "I don't know how much more of this I can stand."

"You're doing fine."

"There's no one to trust. James plans to deceive Mr. Moon and Mr. Moon plans to deceive him. And what was that business about Esther?"

"You can trust me," Fargo said.

Gretchen raised her face to his. "I sensed that from the very beginning. There's something about you."

"Do you still want to go back?"

"Now more than ever. I have to know. I have to talk to her myself and hear her with my own ears."

"You won't like what you hear," Fargo predicted.

"I dare say I won't. But I won't believe it if I don't. I owe her that much. You see that, don't you?"

"I take it you don't want to wait until daybreak?"

"I'd rather not, if it's all the same to you."

Fargo held the Ovaro to a walk. Gretchen sat straight and didn't utter a word the entire ride. He reined off the road when Kill Creek came into sight and went a few yards in among the trees before drawing rein. "We go on foot from here."

Gretchen slid off. "In case I don't have the chance later, I want to thank you for doing this for me."

Fargo pulled the Henry from the scabbard. He levered a round into the chamber, cradled the rifle in his arms, and said, "I told you before. I'm not doing this for you. I'm doing it for me."

"You want to pay them back. Yes, I remember." Gretchen put her hand on the Henry's barrel. "Wait a minute. Surely you don't intend to march in there and shoot them all dead."

"No," Fargo said. "I aim to sneak in and shoot them all dead. Except maybe for one." He was thinking of Serilda.

"Does that include Esther and the redhead? What was her name again? Maxine?"

"They're on the list." Fargo turned to go but she gripped his sleeve.

"Hold on. That would be murder."

"No. That would be stopping them from murdering us."

"But don't you see? If you shoot them, you're no better than they are."

"I never claimed I was." Fargo went to go but she stepped in front of him, blocking his way.

"Please."

"Don't do this. Damn it."

"Do what you want with Moon and James and the others but don't harm Esther."

Fargo stared at her.

"As a personal favor. I want to deal with her."

"She'll stab you in the back."

Gretchen refused to give up. "If she does it's on my shoulders. So will you or won't you?"

Fargo sighed. "I won't make any promises. But if you want her, she's yours so long as she doesn't come after me before you get to her."

"Thank you." Gretchen gazed toward Kill Creek. No light glowed in any of the buildings. "How can people do this to one another?" she sadly asked. "Killing is *wrong*. It's evil."

"Tell that to the Almighty."

"Excuse me?"

"I was on a stage once with a parson. It rained, and after the rain stopped there was a rainbow. The parson went on and on about how it was a sign from God. How God once drowned every last person on the face of the Earth except for Noah and his family, and the rainbow was God's promise that God wouldn't ever do it again."

"I've read that, yes. A wonderful tale."

"Except for all those people God drowned. I asked the parson how many it was and he said he didn't rightly know. Maybe hundreds of thousands. Maybe millions."

"What's your point?"

"You say it's wrong to kill. Yet the Almighty is the biggest killer of them all."

Gretchen smiled. "You're forgetting. One of the Ten Commandments is that we should never, ever kill."

"And who gave us those Commandments?"

"God did, through Moses."

"The same God who drowned all those millions?"

"Yes, but . . ."

"No buts about it. If killing is good enough for God, it's good enough for me."

"You trouble me at times."

"Let's get this over with." Fargo walked around her. The wind had died and the night was still.

His elbow acquired a shapely shadow. "When this is over I'd like to talk to you some more."

"When this is over the last thing I'll want to do is talk. Now hush. There are still two of those dogs left and they have good ears."

Fargo slowed as he neared the stable. He wasn't going to be taken by surprise again if he could help it. Sidling along the wall to the double doors, he peered in.

Gretchen was behind him. In the dark she misjudged and bumped his arm.

"Sorry," she whispered.

"If I asked you to wait in the stage until I say it's safe, would you?"

"You can't get rid of me. Sorry."

The saloon was next. Fargo didn't go in; it appeared to be empty. He moved on.

"Where is everyone?"

Fargo was wondering the same thing. He passed the general store and a house and suddenly Gretchen grabbed the back of his shirt.

"What's that?"

Ahead, a four-legged form stood in the middle of the street. A form that was all too familiar.

"One of the dogs."

"Look behind us," Gretchen said.

Fargo did. The other mastiff was in front of the saloon.

"What will they do?"

"Die." Fargo raised the Henry but he didn't shoot. Not yet. It was too dark to be sure he would bring them down. He might wound them and a wounded animal was twice as dangerous.

"What are you waiting for?"

"For them to come closer."

"Is that smart? That dog in the woods got close and it almost killed you. Shoot now while you can."

"When they rush us, run into that house." Fargo pointed. "Slam the door and find a place to hide."

"Maybe we're fretting over nothing. Maybe they won't attack."

As if they had heard, both mastiffs started toward them.

18

Fargo sighted on the dog coming from the direction of the stable. He took a deep breath and held it to steady his aim. The dog was in a crouch and gave out a menacing growl.

"Skye," Gretchen said anxiously. She had her revolver pointed at the other one.

"Let them get closer," Fargo advised. "So close, we can't miss."

A sharp whistle pierced the air, seeming to come from everywhere at once, and instantly the two dogs whirled and ran between buildings. Within moments they loped out of sight.

"Thank goodness," Gretchen said. "The teeth on those things. They could rip us to pieces."

Fargo suspected that Maxine was watching them and had called off her darlings to spare them from taking lead. But she was well hid.

"Where could everyone have gone? You don't suppose that awful Bromley has killed all of them, do you?"

"Not likely."

"Should we go down into the tunnels and look for them?"

"Not if we can help it." Fargo had been lucky to escape the tunnels alive the first time. He wasn't eager to tempt fate again.

"What then?"

"We do as I wanted to do in the first place. We wait until daylight." Fargo moved across the street toward the bluffs but only went a dozen feet and stopped. "Right here will do."

"Out in the open like this?"

Fargo faced the buildings and sank down cross-legged. "No one can get at us without me seeing." Especially not the dogs.

"But the wind. It will get quite chilly before the night is done. I'd rather we were in the dress shop."

"The same dress shop Esther was taken from?"

Reluctantly, Gretchen folded her legs under her and glumly placed her elbows on her legs and her chin in her hand. "I won't be able to stay awake all night. I'm exhausted."

"You don't have to. I will." Fargo patted his lap. "Here's your pillow when you're ready to sleep."

"My noble protector," Gretchen said, and grinned.

"Noble, hell."

"Do you mind if we talk?"

"About what?" Fargo asked while scanning the shadowed nooks and crannies. He could practically feel unseen eyes on them.

"About you. About why you say you don't ever want to settle down. About what it would take to change your mind."

"Pick something else."

"You're prickly about your feelings. Or is it that you're afraid to admit you need someone to love as much as the next person?"

God spare him from women who believed they had all the answers, Fargo reflected. He decided to set her straight. "That's just it. I don't. I'm content with my life as it is."

"Oh, come on. Endless wandering can't compare to having a loving companion to warm your bed at night."

"I meet plenty of bed warmers. Most I like. But love hardly ever enters into it."

"Wait. Did I understand you correctly? You would go to bed with a woman you didn't like?"

"If a female wants to part her legs for me, I'm more than willing to oblige her."

"Is that all we are to you? Don't you feel guilty afterward?"

"Why should I? It's not like I rape them. I never bed a woman who doesn't want me to bed her."

"How gallant of you," Gretchen said wryly. "So where do I stand in your scheme of things? Did you do it with me because you like me or because I happened to be handy?"

"You chatter like a chipmunk, but other than that, you're a right fine lady," Fargo hedged.

"Thank you. I think." She fell silent.

Fargo could feel the wind on his skin through the rips and tears in his buckskins. He had a spare shirt and pants in his saddlebags but he wouldn't change until this was over with.

After a while Gretchen yawned and said sleepily, "I think I'll take you up on that offer of your lap."

Fargo shifted and held his arms up. She curled on her side and placed her cheek on his thigh and smiled up at him.

"You're a decent man at heart. Do you know that?"

"Don't start."

"I'm serious. You act all tough but here you are safe-guarding someone who by your own admission doesn't mean much more to you than a toss in the hay."

"You keep forgetting I owe them."

"Ah. You want me to think you're out for revenge and nothing else. All right. I'll play along."

Fargo sighed. It had been his experience that most people would think what they wanted to think, even when what they were thinking was dead wrong. They went through life with blinders on and nothing anyone could say or do would make them take the blinders off.

"I heard that. You're a typical man."

"Never claimed to be anything else." Fargo caught a hint of motion in a window. No face appeared, though.

Gretchen closed her eyes and placed her hand under her cheek and the other on her leg. "This is more comfortable than I expected. You have a nice lap."

"Women say the damnedest things."

"Wake me if the dogs show up. I'll cover your back so they can't jump you from behind."

Fargo stroked her hair. That one comment made up for much of her silliness. "Sleep, wench."

"Yes, sir." Gretchen giggled. "I'm afraid you have spoiled me, though. When I get back to civilization, I'll be much more selective."

"What in God's name are you talking about?"

"Men. Refined gentlemen like James and Roy can't hold a candle to you. They're like infants who were never weaned. You, on the other hand, are strong and forceful and confident. Everything a woman looks for."

"Do me a favor and shut up. You keep making more of me than there is. I do what I have to and that's all."

"Some men don't even do that."

Fargo was glad when she didn't say more. Soon her regular breathing told him she had finally fallen asleep. He settled down for a long night. The minutes became snails. It didn't help that he had to constantly stay alert. A lapse could prove fatal.

At one point Fargo swore he heard the patter of running feet but they stopped and he didn't hear them again. Toward the middle of the night a howl wavered eerily from under the ground.

Fargo's eyelids became heavy with fatigue. He had been through a lot since he arrived in Kill Creek and had little chance to rest. Along about four in the morning, he was so weary his chin kept dipping and his eyelids kept drooping.

Each time he shook his head and stretched and willed himself to stay awake.

His chin dipped yet again and his eyes closed and Fargo told himself to open them. The next he knew, a gust of chill wind gave him a start. He jerked his head up and looked around, appalled he had dozed off. By the positions of the stars, he hadn't slept long but it was a mistake he dared not repeat.

"Damn me," Fargo grumbled under his breath so as not to awaken Gretchen.

He gave his head a vigorous toss and his gaze happened to alight on the roof of the general store. *Someone was up there, watching them.* The huge bulk left no doubt who. Fargo started to bring up the Henry but the moment he moved, the shape vanished.

It made Fargo's skin crawl to think that Bromley could have snuck up on him while he slept and bashed his brains out as the madman had bashed out Shorty's. He had no trouble staying awake from then on. Gradually the sky to the east lightened and a golden bank framed the horizon. Off in the forest the birds welcomed the approaching dawn with chirps and warbles and twitters.

Gretchen stirred and rolled onto her back. Her eyes opened and she glanced about in confusion then saw his face and smiled. "I was having the most pleasant dream. You were being very naughty."

"Tell me about it when this is over." Fargo would see to it her dream came true.

Sitting up, Gretchen fussed with her bonnet and then looked down at her dress and frowned. "I'm a mess. I need a bath. I need to wash my hair. I need to change into different clothes. Let's go to the millinery, can we?"

Fargo had no objection. "As soon as the sun is up."

"It's light enough to see now."

"Sunup," Fargo repeated.

"I do wish—" Gretchen began, and stopped, her eyes widening in surprise at something she saw past him.

Fargo twisted and raised the Henry but lowered it again. "You."

"Me," Serilda echoed. She had on the same clothes as before and her revolver was tucked at her waist. She came up and said, "Leave Kill Creek right this minute."

"Where's your pa?" Fargo asked.

"I don't rightly know. He moves around a lot. He'd be mad as hell if he knew I was here. Now please. For the last time. Go while you still can."

Gretchen had recovered from her surprise. "I'm not going anywhere without my friend Esther. Where is she? What have you done to her?"

"Me, nothing," Serilda said. "I'm not out to hurt anyone. It's best you forget about her and just go."

Fargo said, "It's too late for that even if we wanted to."

"For your own good. It's not just my pa you have to worry about. My sister is mad as hell about you killing one of her dogs. . . ."

"Two," Fargo amended.

"Oh God. Now she'll want you dead even more. Unless you're hankering to be torn apart, you'd best light a shuck."

"You haven't told us about my friend Esther," Gretchen said.

"It's too late for her and for those fellas she was with. They snuck down into the tunnels last night, playing right into his hands."

"Your father's?"

"Moon's."

"They're all underground?" Fargo said.

Serilda nodded. "I don't know if you know it but Moon and my sister are stuck on one another. What she sees in him I can't imagine but about a year ago he strayed into Kill Creek and she took a fancy to him. It's why he brought those city folks here. To dispose of after he gets the money."

"So we've heard," Gretchen said. "And you had no hand in any of this?"

"If I did, do you think I'd bother warning you off? I can't stand Moon but what I think doesn't count for a hill of beans with Maxine. She does as she pleases. It's that wild streak of hers."

"Where's Esther?"

"I told you. She went down under. Moon talked them into it. Now they're in a pit and Moon and my sis are making cows' eyes."

Fargo thought to ask, "Conklin?"

"He's down there, too. Keeps looking at me like I'm a slab of beef and he's starved. But he knows I'll shoot him if he so much as lays a finger on me."

"I talked to your pa last night," Fargo said, which was one way of putting it. "He accused me of being after his treasure."

"He accuses everybody of the same. He murdered a priest once, a kindly old man who couldn't have cared less about the mine."

"He's loco, you know. I saw his treasure. It's fool's gold."

A haunted look came into Serilda's eyes. "It was the accident. He was never the same after that beam fell on him. Before, he was a good enough pa. He treated us kindly and we never starved although we hardly ever had more than five dollars in our poke. His big dream was to strike it rich. He dragged us from one gold strike to the next but he could never find any for himself. Then we came here and our world went to hell."

"Why didn't you leave Kill Creek when everyone else did?" Gretchen asked.

"Pa refused. He was sure the gold hadn't played out and he'd find a new vein that would make us rich. We'd almost got him convinced when a tunnel caved in. It took us months to nurse him back to health. Wasn't long after that he found his treasure. Maxine and me didn't have the heart to tell him it was fool's gold. I doubt he'd believe us anyway." Serilda put a hand over her eyes. "It's been a living nightmare."

"When we do go you should come with us," Fargo suggested.

Serilda lowered her hand. "I can't desert him no matter how crazy he is. Nor Maxine, as much as I might like to. Blood counts for more than anything. So please. Leave."

"Can't." Fargo stood and arched his back to relieve a

cramp. "I'm going underground. Since you won't help, stay out of my way."

"Who says I won't?"

"You will lend us a hand?" From Gretchen.

"Since you're being so pigheaded, I'll take you to your friend and those two gents. But mark my words. Go down into those tunnels and there's a good chance you'll never come back up."

"Why should we trust you?"

"Because I don't want my pa or my sister hurt. I will do anything to see they aren't. I'll get you in and out quick and then you can be on your way."

"That's good enough for me."

It wasn't good enough for Fargo but all he said was, "Lead the way."

19

Serilda made for the bluffs. She acted nervous and was constantly glancing every which way.

"Why don't we go down one of the trapdoors in the buildings?" Fargo was curious to learn.

"There's too much chance of running into Pa. His treasure room, as he calls it, isn't far from the saloon." Serilda nodded at the bluffs. "He doesn't come out this way much. All the ore was taken out long ago."

"And Esther?" Gretchen asked. "You still haven't said exactly where she is?"

"I have to show you."

Fargo was mildly surprised when they crossed the stream and even more surprised when Serilda went around a boulder the size of a covered wagon and brought them to a typical mine entrance with heavy timbers for supports and a crossbeam. He'd had no idea it was there.

"This is where the mine got its start," Serilda disclosed as she stopped to take a lantern off a peg. "The vein they were following branched and then branched again. They dug and dug until they found the mother lode. It turned out to be under Kill Creek. There was big talk that it was the richest vein ever found, but it played out. They always do." She lit the lantern. "Stay close. We should be able to reach your friends without my pa catching on if we're real quiet."

"Thank you for your help," Gretchen said.

Serilda gave her a strange glance. "Think nothing of it. I'd do the same for anyone."

Fargo let them go ahead so he could watch behind them. He was wary of a trick. The tunnel ran straight for about a hundred yards and then forked. Serilda took the left branch. Almost immediately the tunnel narrowed to where the sides brushed his shoulders.

"I don't like being closed in," Gretchen remarked. "Why couldn't we stay in the other part?"

"My pa never uses this tunnel," Serilda said over her shoulder. "My sister neither."

Fargo looked down. Tracks besides their own were imprinted in the dust underfoot. He couldn't tell how long the tracks had been there but plainly she wasn't telling the truth. They went around a bend. The tunnel widened to six feet across but only for a short way. Beyond, it narrowed again.

Serilda stopped and faced them. "Why don't you two wait here while I go scout ahead?"

"Stop her," Fargo said, and tried to get past Gretchen but she chose that moment to turn into his path. "Move!"

"Why? What's wrong?"

Fargo went to shove her aside. He saw Serilda kick at a support. Precariously balanced, it gave out. Above them, a beam split with a loud *crack*. He grabbed Gretchen and whirled to run but a torrent of dirt rained down. Gretchen cried out as the force of the cascading earth smashed them to the ground. He threw his arms over his head and face as the earth kept falling and falling. Then, as abruptly as it began, the brown rain stopped.

Coughing and swiping at the choking cloud of dust, Fargo raised his head. He was pinned, covered with dirt from his shoulders to his boots. Beside him Gretchen wheezed and gagged. They were lucky. If the dirt had covered them completely, they'd have smothered.

From behind them came Serilda's quiet, "I'm sorry."

"Why?" Gretchen asked between coughs. "Why did you do this?"

"I told you. I don't want my pa or my sister hurt. I gave you your chance to leave but you wouldn't take it."

Gretchen was trying to rise and couldn't. "We're trapped. You can't leave us like this. We'll starve or die of thirst."

"My pa will find you long before that happens. He'll finish you off. Either crush your skulls or strangle you."

"Oh God," Gretchen said. "Please. Dig us out. We'll go away. I give you my word."

"And desert your dear friend Esther?" Serilda said sarcastically. "No, I'm afraid you've dug your own graves. Again, I'm sorry it had to be this way. I truly am."

"Wait!"

The light faded, plunging them in darkness.

"Skye? Why didn't you say anything?"

Fargo pushed up against the dirt. He managed to rise a hair but no more.

"Say something, will you?"

"I liked her." Fargo's right hand was flat under him but his left was out to the side and twisted from the fall. He wriggled his wrist, loosening the dirt's grip so he could pull his arm toward him.

Gretchen was struggling to free herself. "It's hopeless. There must be tons of dirt on top of us."

"If there was we'd be crushed." A few hundred pounds was Fargo's guess, most of it on their lower backs and legs. He worked at his left hand and presently had it flat on the ground, too.

"What are you doing? I can't tell."

"Hush."

"You say that a lot."

"Because you talk too damn much." Fargo bunched his shoulders and arms and heaved upward. He rose barely half an inch. Sinking back down, he gathered his strength for another try.

"You suspected she would try something, didn't you?"

"So much for being quiet." Fargo pushed. This time his shoulders rose an inch.

"I'm afraid, darn you. It helps if I talk. Haven't you ever been afraid?"

"Not so I couldn't stop flapping my gums." Fargo tried again. He rose hardly higher than before. At this rate, he'd be at it most of the day. That wouldn't do. "Can you move any?"

"My right arm, a little. My legs feel numb. I hope to God they aren't broken."

Fargo tried something new. He braced both forearms and levered forward, pushing with his feet as he did. Dirt fell on either side of him. He tried harder, his teeth clenched.

"Did you hear something?"

Fargo stopped and listened. The tunnels were as still as a graveyard. "What was it?"

"A sound."

"Maybe it was a rat."

"Please tell me that was a joke. I detest mice and I am terrified of rats. I can't stand to be near them."

"Keep talking and you'll bring them right to us."

That shut her up. Fargo continued his efforts to extricate them. He had dirt in his eyes and in his nose and he could taste dirt in his mouth by the time he freed his shoulders and stopped to rest.

"You were jesting about the rats, weren't you?"

Fargo grunted.

"That was unkind. I think you owe me..." Gretchen stopped. "There. I know I heard a sound that time."

So did Fargo, the ponderous tread of heavy feet, faint but coming closer.

He surged up and out, throwing all he had into breaking free. More dirt slid off of him. He twisted his hips and pulled his legs but from the waist down he was still pinned. The footsteps were nearer. In desperation he tugged and twisted.

He broke out in sweat and his legs screamed in protest.

Suddenly his hips were free. He stopped again and cocked his head.

The footsteps had stopped. Or was it that whoever was coming down the tunnel had heard him and was stalking forward with the stealth of an Apache?

It had to be Bromley. Fargo knew there would be no reasoning with the madman. Either he freed himself or they were both as good as dead. Turning, he clawed at the dirt with both hands.

"Skye!" Gretchen whispered, aghast.

A huge bulk filled the opening, a darker black that towered over them like a great bear.

Fargo had dropped the Henry when the roof caved in and figured it was buried. He stabbed his hand for his Colt—and found an empty holster. When the dirt smashed him flat it had knocked the Colt loose.

The bulk bent until the hood was inches from Fargo's face and fetid breath fanned him. "Brom remember you. You want his treasure."

"We're trapped," Fargo said. "Help free us."

Gruff mirth boomed from the barrel chest. "You funny man, thief. Brom not help. Brom kill."

An iron hand clamped on Fargo's shirt, and he was wrenched upward so savagely, it was a wonder his spine didn't snap.

"You stupid to come back. You stupidest man ever."

Fargo pried at the lunatic's fingers but they were like metal spikes. "I did it to help your daughter, Serilda."

"What about Brom's girl?" Brom rumbled.

"She's in trouble. Her and Maxine, both. There are bad men in your tunnels. They aim to kill them."

"Moon," Brom spat.

"You know about him? Then you know he can't be trusted."

"Moon want Maxine. Brom tell her no but she not listen. She never listen to Brom."

"She needs you to protect her. You better go to her."

The monstrous ruin seemed to be studying him. "Brom think maybe you lie. Brom think maybe you try to trick him."

"Ask her," Fargo said, motioning at Gretchen. "She will tell you Moon is out to kill your girls."

Gretchen had caught on to Fargo's ploy. "Yes. He's right. I heard Moon say so. Go to them before it's too late."

Bromley fell quiet save for his raspy breathing. Then he rumbled, "Brom believe you."

"Good," Fargo said.

"But Brom not free you. Brom keep you here."

Fargo never saw the blow. His head exploded with pain and he thought he heard Gretchen scream and then a dark well sucked him into its depths.

He drifted in a limbo of nausea and vertigo until a squeak and the patter of small feet on his face brought him up out of the well with a start that sent new pain shooting from his head to his toes.

Fargo groaned. Whatever had squeaked, squeaked again, and the small feet pattered off. A rat, he reckoned. He marveled that he was still alive. Maybe his skull was harder than Shorty's. Or maybe in the dark Brom had misjudged the blow.

Fargo took stock. He was woozy and half sick and his legs were still pinned but he was breathing. "Gretchen?" He reached out—and she wasn't there, only dirt. "Gretchen?" he shouted, and the truth hit him as hard as Brom's punch.

The lunatic had taken her.

Fargo pulled on his legs but had to stop after a few seconds. His head swam and his gut flipped and flopped like a fish out of water. He was still until it stopped and then he twisted and dug at the dirt like a man possessed, throwing it from him as fast as he could. His fingers smacked something hard, stinging them. He ran his hand over it, and smiled. He had found the Colt.

Fargo kept at it. Every now and then he pulled on his

legs but he wasn't able to budge them until, after much too long, he gave a hard wrench, and he was free. Rising to his knees, he felt about for the Henry. He was worried it was buried and he'd have to come back with a lantern and a shovel.

More dizziness prompted him to sit and rest. He extended his legs and his right boot bumped a rock. Or was it? He leaned and groped and smiled a second time. Now he had the Henry, too.

His hat hadn't felt right since the rat brought him back to the world of the living. He hadn't bothered with it but now he reached up and discovered the crown had been crumpled flat by Bromley's blow. He took it off and restored it to its normal shape and jammed it back on.

Fargo rose. He half expected his head to spin but it didn't and he felt his way to the narrow tunnel and then along it to where it branched. He turned left.

Eventually, if his sense of direction hadn't failed him, it would bring him to the main tunnel under Kill Creek.

Fargo moved with grim resolve. He wasn't holding back any longer. Serilda's treachery had been the last straw. He had wanted to spare her if he could, but no longer.

The darkness, the rustling of the rats, had no effect on him. Fire burned in his veins, a molten thirst for vengeance on those who had done their damnedest to put him under the ground, permanent.

From far down the tunnel came a scream. It sounded like Gretchen.

Fargo moved faster but he hurried only a short way and caught himself. He couldn't help her if he blundered into another pit or some other trap Brom had rigged.

The passageway seemed endless.

Suddenly Fargo was struck on the shoulder. Startled, he sprang back and raised the Henry but no one was there. At least, not that he could see, and he couldn't see much in all that black.

When nothing else happened, he warily moved forward, swinging the rifle from side to side. His shoulder bumped something that stuck out of the wall and it made a creaking noise. He reached up. For once things were going his way. It was a lantern on a peg.

Fargo gave it a shake. The tank was about half full. He raised the glass and lit the wick and moved on.

It wouldn't be long now.

Bromley and his girls and Moon and his gun sharks didn't know it yet but hell was coming to call.

Fargo was out for blood.

20

Fargo hadn't gone that far when another scream pierced the dank tunnel air. Throwing caution aside, he ran. Traps or no traps, if that was Gretchen, she needed help. He flew around a bend and had to dig in his boot heels to keep from colliding with someone coming from the other direction.

"You!" Conklin blurted. He was holding a lantern and a rifle, too. He made no move to raise the rifle, which was pointed at the ground.

Fargo's Henry was pointed down, as well. He stood waiting, his every muscle as taut as wire.

"The girl said she'd taken care of you," Conklin said. "Something about a cave-in."

"Where's Gretchen?"

"Haven't seen her for hours," Conklin said. "Moon sent me to make sure you were dead."

"Too bad he didn't come himself."

"You can't beat him. He's too quick." Conklin squared his thin shoulders. "I'm no slouch myself."

"I figured you would try. Give my regards to Tucker and Beck when you see them."

"Where are they, anyhow?"

"Waiting for you in hell."

Conklin glanced at the Henry and a sly smile curled his lips.

Fargo could guess why. The Henry's hammer wasn't

thumbed back. The hammer on Conklin's Spencer was. Conklin thought he had an edge.

"Moon will be mighty disappointed. He wanted to buck you out himself. Me, I want that horse of yours. It's a fine animal."

"Take it if you think you're man enough."

A flush of anger spread from Conklin's collar to his hat.

"Whenever you're ready."

"Ladies first."

Conklin swore and started to swing the Spencer up.

Fargo was ready. He threw his lantern at Conklin's face while simultaneously hiking the Henry and thumbing back the hammer. Conklin had instinctively ducked. The lantern hit him high on the head and shattered just as he snapped off a shot. Flame leaped, and he missed. Fargo didn't. He shot Conklin smack between the eyes. The heavy slug burst out the rear of Conklin's head and the lanky gunman fell in a heap.

Fargo snatched Conklin's lantern as Conklin was going down. Stepping over the body, he ran. Soon a fork appeared. He took the one that he thought would take him under Kill Creek. He was moving so fast that he almost didn't see a side passage. Slowing, he sidled toward it.

Out of the shadows stepped Serilda, her hand on her revolver. "You're a hard man to stop."

"You shouldn't have done that," Fargo said.

"They are my pa and my sister. I told you I wouldn't let you hurt them. I practically begged you to leave, but no."

"Let it go."

"I can't," Serilda said sadly. "I wish to God I could but I can't let you go any farther."

"Back off."

"The only way is for you to drop your rifle and that pistol and I promise you can leave unharmed. I'll even walk you to your horse."

"He took Gretchen."

"I know."

"It doesn't have to be like this."

"Yes, it does. I'm sorry, truly sorry. I like you. I like you a lot. I figure if we'd met somewhere else, we'd have good times together. It's a pity."

"Don't," Fargo said.

"You won't have to feel guilty if it's you who lives."

"Damn you."

"Funny, isn't it? The things we do for our family, even when we don't want to?" Serilda smiled. "So long, handsome." She jerked her six-gun.

Fargo tried the same trick—he hurled the lantern at her face. She was quicker than Conklin and sidestepped and had her revolver up and out before he could reach her. It thundered and a searing pain lanced his side. Dropping the Henry, he grabbed the Smith and Wesson by the barrel and shoved it away from him. It went off again, into the wall. She clawed at his eyes and he got hold of her other wrist and sought to trip her but she was too nimble. Her knee arced at his groin but caught his thigh instead. She drove her forehead at his face. He managed to take the blow on his cheek but it still hurt like hell.

Serilda fought frantically to break his grip. "I won't let you hurt them!" she shouted, and tried to sink her teeth into his neck.

Fargo slugged her. He let go of her wrist and punched her full on the jaw, and he didn't hold back. It rocked her onto her heels and left her in a heap at his feet, blood trickling from a corner of her mouth. Working quickly, he drew his Arkansas toothpick and cut strips from her shirt. He tied her wrists and her ankles and for extra measure stuffed a gag in her mouth. "That should hold you."

The lantern hadn't broken and lay on its side. Scooping it up, he examined his side. The slug had left a furrow but spared his ribs. He retrieved the Henry and jogged on down the tunnel. They would suspect he was coming and be ready for him. So be it.

Fargo thought the next obstacle would be Moon but he was mistaken. He came to a straight stretch and there she was at the other end in all her wild redheaded glory, her hands on her hips, a mastiff on either side, a pistol in her belt. Unlike her sister there was no sadness in her eyes or regret in her features. There was only pure hate.

Fargo stopped.

"Did you kill her?"

"No."

"That's something, at least," Maxine said. "You killed two of my dogs, though, you son of a bitch."

"They were trying to kill me."

Maxine advanced several steps and the mastiffs moved with her, their hackles bristling, their fangs bared. "They were my friends. I wouldn't expect you to understand but until Moon came along they were all I had. They went with me everywhere. They did everything I did. They mean more to me than my pa or my sister. They sure as hell mean more to me than you." She glanced down and cried fiercely, "Get him!" Both mastiffs bounded forward and she came after them, drawing her six-shooter.

Fargo dropped into a crouch and set the lantern down. He wedged the Henry to his shoulder and took a swift bead and blew out the brains of the dog on the right. Working the lever, he fed a new cartridge into the chamber and aimed at the second dog. It was incredibly fast. It was almost to him when he stroked the trigger. He was sure he hit it but it didn't slow. He threw up his arms and it plowed into him, bowling him over. Quick as a cat he scrambled into a crouch and palmed the Colt but the mastiff was on its side, twitching and convulsing, blood seeping from a hole high in its chest.

"Nooooooooo!"

The screech saved Fargo's life. He spun as Maxine's revolver cracked and the slug buzzed his ear. She fired again but she was hasty. Fargo was more deliberate. He shot her in the face.

His ears ringing, Fargo reloaded. He slid the Colt into his holster, reclaimed the lantern and the Henry, and moved on. Another fifty yards brought him to a side tunnel. He was passing it when he heard voices and a sob.

Fargo entered the passage. A sharp bend hid whatever lay beyond. Another sob warned him he was close.

"Please. I can't take the pain," Esther pleaded. "You can't let me suffer like this. It's inhuman."

No one answered her.

"Say something. Damn you!" James Harker roared.

"It's no use," Roy Landreth said. "He's shown his true colors. We were fools to trust him."

Fargo had a good idea who they were talking about. Ready to shoot, he risked a quick look-see.

Another chamber had been carved from the earth. A pit took up most of it.

Quartz glistened in the walls, illuminated by a lantern on the ground near the pit's edge. On the far side a dark opening led into another tunnel. Partway around, at the base of the wall, lay Roy Landreth's cane.

"Are you still up there?" James Harker hollered.

The chamber was empty. Fargo cat-stepped around the bend and over to the hole. He set his lantern next to the other and asked, "Who are you talking to?"

James and Landreth were bent over Esther. Straightening, they spun and gaped in astonishment. James was the first to find his voice.

"Moon. We were talking to Moon. Isn't he up there? He was just a minute ago."

"Get us out of here," Landreth said. "Find a rope, a ladder, anything. Esther needs doctoring. Both her wrists are broken."

The cause of all the bloodshed and sorrow was on her back, her face as pale as a bedsheet, her arms on her belly, each bent unnaturally. Grimacing, she said, "When they threw us in, I landed wrong."

"I tried setting her bones but it made her scream," James said.

"Where's Gretchen?" Fargo had figured she was with them.

"We haven't seen her since last evening," James replied, and poked a finger at him. "Why are you still standing there? Do something."

"How did you get down here?"

Roy Landreth responded. "Moon brought us down at gunpoint. Apparently he intended to betray us all along and keep the money for himself. Now quit asking stupid questions and help us out."

"Where did he get to?"

"I'm right behind you," Moon said.

Fargo froze.

"Toss the rifle and turn. Nice and slow or I'll shoot you where you stand."

As much as Fargo wanted to settle accounts, he complied.

Moon had a Remington in each hand. "Smart man. You get to live a little while." He moved so his back was to the wall. "Seen any sign of Bromley?"

"Not for a while." Fargo was puzzled by why Moon hadn't shot him dead. "He got hold of Gretchen."

From the pit came Landreth's wail of, "God, no."

Moon frowned and said, "I should have shot that loco son of a bitch long ago. But I spared him for her sake." He paused. "Maxine, not the other one. Me and her have become real close."

"So I've heard."

"She's a wildcat, that gal. Why she fancies me I'll never know. You'd think she would go for a gent like those dandies in the pit. Someone who wears fine clothes and has good manners." Moon chuckled. "Listen to me. We should get to it. But first I need to know. Tucker and Beck. Where are they?"

"Dead."

"I heard shots a while ago. Was that Conklin and you, by any chance?"

"He's dead too."

"Damn. But that means more money for me."

Fargo was stunned by what Moon did next: he twirled the Remingtons into their holsters and patted them. "What's this?"

"What do you think it is?"

"You're that sure of yourself?"

Moon nodded. "It will give me something to brag about, how I shot the great scout in a fair fight."

"I have something to brag about too."

"What would that be?"

"I shot Maxine."

Moon visibly shook. "You're just saying that to rattle me."

"You'll find her back up the tunnel. But you better hurry. There might not be much left after the rats get done."

Moon uttered a sharp cry and his hands became twin lightning bolts. So were Fargo's. He fired as Moon cleared leather. He fired as Moon banged off two shots. He fired as Moon staggered, and he fired again as Moon pitched to his knees and yet again as Moon's arms sagged limp at his sides. Fargo raised the Colt. "I shot her in the face," he said, and did the same to Moon.

"Is he dead?" James called up.

"They don't get any deader." Fargo was almost finished. Only one thing left to do. He turned toward the pit and froze a second time.

In the tunnel opening in the other side stood Bromley. His hood was pulled back, his features hideous. Gretchen was belly-down over his shoulder, and she wasn't moving.

"Did Brom hear right? You killed Brom's girl?" Throwing Gretchen down, the madman hurtled around the pit, moving incredibly fast for someone so huge.

Fargo's fingers flew to his belt. The Colt was empty. He realized he wouldn't be able to reload before the brute reached him, and spun toward the Henry. Diving, he swept it into his hands and turned to shoot but a living avalanche slammed into him and he was flung against the wall so hard, it was a wonder every bone in his body didn't shatter. A calloused hand knocked the Henry from his grasp. A fist caught him in the pit of his stomach and drove him to his knees.

Howling in fury, Brom gripped Fargo by the throat and shook him as a grizzly might shake a marmot. "Brom kill you! Brom kill you for killing Brom's girl!"

By then Fargo's hand was out of his boot. "Kill this," he said, and thrust the toothpick into Brom's right eye. The razor-sharp steel sliced through the eyeball and deep into the socket. Brom stiffened and his maw of a mouth grew wide but all he did was gasp, and die.

Fargo yanked the toothpick out. "Thoughtful of you to dig your own grave," he said, and kicked him in the chest. Like a tall tree in the forest, the deformed lunatic toppled back and went over the edge. There was a crash and a shriek and then silence.

Fargo moved to the edge.

James and Landreth were statues. Sprawled between them was Brom's bulk. Esther's head poked from under Brom's shoulder, her face nearly purple, her tongue lolling, as lifeless as the creature who had unwittingly crushed her.

Collecting his pistol and rifle, Fargo hastened around the pit. The two men shouted but he ignored them. Reaching Gretchen, he knelt and slowly rolled her over, dreading what he would find. Her right cheek was puffy and she had a large bruise on her brow. He gently shook her.

Gretchen groaned. Her eyes opened, and she said softly, "You saved me again?"

"It's a long ride to San Francisco and I can use the company."

Gretchen laughed but caught herself. "God, I hurt all over. And I'm so tired."

"Rest." Fargo scooped her into his arms and retraced his

steps to the tunnel he came out of. Along the way he helped himself to a lantern. As he was about to leave, James Harker bellowed his name.

"Where are you going? You can't leave us down here. We'll starve to death."

"Maybe you can get the stage driver to bring you some food."

Fargo carried Gretchen to the main tunnel. She had passed out and he let her rest. When he reached Serilda he set Gretchen down, drew his toothpick and turned to cut Serilda loose. Her back was to him. From her posture he could tell she had struggled to free herself. He put his hand on her shoulder. "Serilda?"

She didn't answer or move.

Fargo eased her onto her back, and swore. Her face was discolored, her eyes wide, her body stiff. In her struggles she had swallowed the gag and choked to death.

Fargo couldn't get out of the tunnels fast enough. He smiled when at last he emerged from the mine entrance and breathed fresh air and felt warm sunlight on his face.

Gretchen stirred and sleepily asked, "How are we doing, handsome?"

"We're doing just fine," Skye Fargo said.

LOOKING FORWARD!
The following is the opening section of the next novel in the exciting *Trailsman* series from Signet:

THE TRAILSMAN #342
ROCKY MOUNTAIN REVENGE

The Rockies, 1860—where the stakes are higher than the mountain peaks, and death crouches in the shadows beside every trail.

Someone was stalking Skye Fargo.

As usual, Fargo was up at the pink tinge of dawn. The mornings were chilly that deep in the Green River country, and the first thing he did was rekindle the fire and put what was left of last night's coffee on. He sat cross-legged, letting the flames warm him, and gazed at the pink to the east.

Fargo's lake blue eyes narrowed. For an instant he thought he saw the silhouette of a rider in the distance. He blinked, and it was gone. He watched for it to reappear and when it didn't he held his hands to the crackling flames and listened to his stomach growl.

Fargo opened his saddlebags. He took out a bundle of

pemmican wrapped in rabbit fur, unwrapped the fur, and bit into a piece.

This was the life Fargo liked best, just him and the Ovaro, wandering where the wind took them. For a while, anyway. His poke was almost empty and soon he must give thought to filling it. Not that he cared all that much about money. If he did, he wouldn't make his living as a scout and tracker and whatever else chance tossed his way.

When the Arbuckle's was hot, Fargo poured a steaming cup full. He held the cup in both hands and sipped and felt it warm him down to his toes. He looked to the east and saw the silhouette again. The rider was coming over the crest of a hill and dipped into dense timber.

Fargo's brow puckered. The rider was coming from the same direction he had. In fact, the rider appeared to be smack on his trail. It could be coincidence but Fargo hadn't survived as long he had by assuming people always had the best of intentions.

He finished the cup and poured another. He usually had two, sometimes more. Coffee cost money and he hated to waste it. By the time he was done the sun was up and the world around him was rosy and warm. He doused the fire and rolled up his blankets. He threw his saddle blanket on the Ovaro and then the saddle. He collected his saddlebags, tied his bedroll, and was ready to ride out.

Fargo checked to the east. The rider wasn't in sight. He forked leather, the saddle creaking under him, lifted the reins, and lightly touched his spurs to the stallion. He rode to the northwest. He was in no particular hurry.

The forest was alive with wildlife. Robins and sparrows and jays warbled and chirped and squawked. Ravens flapped overhead. A startled rabbit bounded away. A pair of does raised their tails and fled in high leaps. A cow elk crashed through the brush, snorting in annoyance at being disturbed.

Fargo climbed to the top of a hill and drew rein. Shifting in the saddle, he stared down at the meadow. In a while, the rider emerged from the trees and went to the exact spot where Fargo had camped. The man dismounted and knelt and put his hands to the embers.

"I'll be damned." So far as Fargo was aware, he didn't have any enemies out to kill him. Not at the moment, anyway. He'd made more than a few. It came from his knack for running into folks who thought they had the god-given right to ride roughshod over everyone else. He couldn't abide that. Step on his toes and there was hell to pay.

Fargo reined around and rode on. He wasn't overly worried.

Whoever was after him was a good tracker but he was in his element. Few knew the wilds as well as he did. Few knew as many tricks to stay alive.

He went about a mile, enough to give the man hunting him the idea that he didn't suspect anything. Then he cast about for a likely spot. An oak tree with a low limb caught his eye. He rode directly under it and went another hundred yards before he drew rein. Swinging down, he tied the Ovaro behind a spruce and shucked his Henry from the saddle scabbard.

Staying well away from the Ovaro's tracks, he returned to the oak. He jumped, caught hold of the low limb, and pulled himself up. Moving to a higher branch, he sat with his back to the bole and put the Henry across his legs.

"Come and get me, you son of a bitch."

The minutes crawled. A squirrel scampered among the tree tops. He was glad it didn't notice him. The racket it would make would alert the rider.

A golden finch and its mate landed on a nearby limb and flew off in alarm when they saw him.

A hoof thudded dully.

Fargo fixed his gaze on the Ovaro's tracks. Off through the trees the rider appeared. A white man in a high-crowned hat and a cowhide vest and a flannel shirt and chaps. In a holster high on the man's right hip was a Starr revolver.

Fargo raised the Henry to his shoulder.

The man appeared to be in his thirties, maybe early forties. He had a square, rugged face sprinkled with stubble. He was broad across the chest and sat the saddle like someone born to it. His gaze was on the ground.

Fargo let the rider get almost to the oak and then he levered a round into the chamber and said, "Tweet, tweet."

The man jerked his head up and drew rein and started to draw but froze when he saw the Henry pointed at him.

"Take your hand off the six-gun."

The man did.

"Raise your arms and keep them where I can see them."

The man did.

"Now give me a good reason why I shouldn't blow out your wick."

"You'd kill a man for nothing?" The rider's voice was deep and low, almost as deep and low as Fargo's.

"Do I look green behind the ears?" Fargo rejoined. "I don't like being hunted. So think fast and make it good." He noticed that the man wasn't tense or anxious or upset. Most would be, with a rifle held on them.

"I have been hunting you, yes."

"You admit it?"

"Why wouldn't I? I don't have anything to hide. I'm not out to do you in, if that's what you're thinking. If I was, you wouldn't have caught on to me."

"Brag a lot, do you?"

The man grinned. "My handle is Stoddard. Jim Stoddard. I work for Clarence Bell of the Circle B. Could be you've heard of him."

"Could be I haven't."

"The Circle B is up to the Sweetwater River country. In ten years it will be the biggest ranch in these or any other parts."

"You ride for the brand?"

"That I do. I'm a puncher. But I hunted a lot as a kid and I'm a fair hand at tracking, so Mr. Bell sent me to find you."

"How in hell did you know I was even in the territory?"

"Mr. Bell had a letter to send east. We went to Sweetwater Station the day after you shot that gent who cheated you at cards."

Fargo sighed. The Central, Overland, California and Pikes Peak Express Company ran a stage line from Saint Louis to Salt Lake City. Sweetwater Station was a stage stop. There was also a saloon. He'd stopped for a drink and a friendly game of cards but the game didn't stay friendly and he had to shoot a two-bit gambler who had a card rig up his sleeve.

"The barkeep told Mr. Bell and mentioned as you were almost as famous as Kit Carson and Jim Bridger."

"Oh, hell."

"Mr. Bell sent me after you and here I am," Stoddard concluded his account. "Now if you'll climb down and fetch your horse, I can take you to the Circle B."

"You're getting ahead of yourself," Fargo told him. The account made sense as far as it went but he still wasn't satisfied and he didn't lower the Henry. "Why does your boss want to see me?"

"To hire you. He says he is willing to pay you a thousand dollars to do him a favor."

Fargo whistled. "It must be some favor." He waited for the cowboy to tell him what it was but Stoddard just sat there. "Is it a secret or am I supposed to guess?"

"I would say if I knew. The boss wants to tell you himself. He did say that he'd give you a hundred dollars just to come hear him out."

"He's awful generous with his money."

"He can afford to be." Stoddard wagged his arms. "Can I put these down? My shoulders are commencing to hurt." He started to do it anyway and stiffened when Fargo sighted down the Henry's barrel. "Hold on. I just explained everything. You have no call to shoot me."

"People don't always tell the truth." Holding the Henry steady, Fargo moved to a lower branch. "Shed the hardware. Use two fingers."

"Damn, you are one suspicious son of a bitch," Stoddard complained, but he slowly plucked the revolver from its holster and bent and let it drop to the grass. "Happy now?"

"Open the vest."

"All I've got under it is my shirt."

"Open it anyway."

Frowning, the cowboy parted the vest wide. "There. I'm not carrying a hideout. I'm no assassin. I punch cows for a living."

Still keeping the Henry on him, Fargo slipped to the lowest branch, perched for a moment with his legs dangling, and dropped. He landed in a crouch on the balls of his feet. Unfurling, he sidled around and picked up the Starr. "I'll hold on to this until I think I can trust you."

"I don't much like you taking my six-shooter. I feel half naked without it."

Fargo sympathized. He would feel the same. "Your boss should have told you what he wants me for. He must have plenty of cowhands working for him—"

"Pretty near thirty."

"Yet he needs me to do him a favor? Why not have one of you do it?"

"I honest to God don't know. The big sugar doesn't confide in me like he does Griff Jackson."

"Who?"

"The foreman. As tough an hombre who ever lived. If Mr. Bell had sent Jackson instead of me, he'd take your rifle and beat you half to death with it."

Fargo moved a few yards behind the cowboy's sorrel. "Ride ahead until we get to my horse. No tricks, hear?"

"Mister, I ain't feather-headed. I get forty a month, and found. That's hardly enough to die for."

Fargo was beginning to like him. "Why don't you tell me a little bit about yourself?"

"What the hell for?"

"To pass the time."

Stoddard muttered something, then declared, "If this don't beat all. Are all of you Daniel Boone's so nosy?"

"The ones who are fond of breathing."

"There's not much to tell. I was raised on a farm in Indiana. I got an itch and drifted west when I was sixteen and did some cow work and liked it. Been at it ever since. Drifted to Denver a while back and Mr. Bell was hiring and I signed on."

"He came all the way up here to start a ranch?" Fargo had heard of a few but there wasn't a town to be had for hundreds of miles and no railhead, either.

"Mr. Bell ain't like you and me. He's always looking to the future. He says as how the country is growing and people are multiplying like rabbits and all of them will need beef to eat."

"He's not worried about Indians? The Bannocks or the Cheyenne or the Arapaho?" All of whom, Fargo knew, had clashed with whites in recent years. The situation was bound to get worse now that the Indians realized the white man intended to claim their land.

"Mr. Bell says it will be a cold day in hell before he'll let redskins or anyone else run him—" Stoddard stopped and straightened and reined up. "Say, is that your animal?"

Fargo looked, and his blood chilled. They were almost to

the spruce. The Ovaro was no longer tied to it. Three men were about to lead it away. Two were on horseback. The third had dismounted to untie the reins and had them in his hand. Fargo stalked toward them. He tossed the Starr to the cowpoke as he went by and snapped, "That's my horse you're stealing."

The three were cut from the same coarse cloth. They weren't white and they weren't red. They were a mix. Their clothes were grubby and they were grubby but their rifles and revolvers looked to be well oiled and their eyes glittered like the eyes of hungry wolves.

The man holding the stallion's reins had a Sharps at his side and bushy eyebrows as big as wooly caterpillars. "It was here by itself," he said. "We reckoned maybe someone left it."

Fargo almost called him a liar to his dirty face. Instead he held out his left hand. "I'll take those."

"Sure, mister." The breed held out the reins. "We don't want trouble. If you say it's yours, it's yours." He turned to climb on his mount.

"Hold on." Fargo was wondering how it was that they happened to be there at the same time as Jim Stoddard. He glanced at the cowboy and saw that Stoddard had holstered the revolver. "You didn't think to holler and see if anyone was around?"

The breed shrugged. "We figured anyone who would leave a fine animal like this must be dead. It's not as if we were following you to steal it."

"That's exactly what they were doing," Jim Stoddard remarked.

Both Fargo and the half-breed looked at him and said, "What?"

"I spotted them yesterday, south of you a ways," the puncher explained. "They were shadowing you and keeping well hid. It's why I rode hard to catch up today. I figured you'd want to know."

"Well, now." Fargo shifted so he could watch all three and said to the man who'd had the reins, "You're a liar as well as a horse thief."

"You're taking his word over mine? Why? Because he's a white and I'm not?"

"No. I'm taking his word because you were fixing to steal my horse, you goddamn idiot."

The man with the caterpillar eyebrows scowled. "I don't take kindly to insults," he said, and dropped his hand to his six-gun.

No other series packs this much heat!

THE TRAILSMAN

#320: OREGON OUTRAGE
#321: FLATHEAD FURY
#322: APACHE AMBUSH
#323: WYOMING DEATHTRAP
#324: CALIFORNIA CRACKDOWN
#325: SEMINOLE SHOWDOWN
#326: SILVER MOUNTAIN SLAUGHTER
#327: IDAHO GOLD FEVER
#328: TEXAS TRIGGERS
#329: BAYOU TRACKDOWN
#330: TUCSON TYRANT
#331: NORTHWOODS NIGHTMARE
#332: BEARTOOTH INCIDENT
#333: BLACK HILLS BADMAN
#334: COLORADO CLASH
#335: RIVERBOAT RAMPAGE
#336: UTAH OUTLAWS
#337: SILVER SHOWDOWN
#338: TEXAS TRACKDOWN
#339: RED RIVER RECKONING
#340: HANNIBAL RISING

**Follow the trail of the gun-slinging heroes of
Penguin's Action Westerns at
penguin.com/actionwesterns**